"[A] subversively clever debut collection . . . angry, at times legitimately scary—demonstrate a subtlety ot purpose that belies [Kupersmith's] youth. . . . The supernatural also helps Kupersmith avoid a common approach among American writers, one in which Vietnam and the Vietnamese act as props to expose America's virtues and flaws. . . . Vietnam remains for many Americans less a place than an idea, the crucible on which the country's imperial ambitions foundered. The inhuman element in her stories leads us away from these clichés, making the characters more human and humane."

—*The New York Times Book Review*

"In perhaps the most pungent story here, a young woman who works the graveyard shift stocking shelves at Kwon's World Grocery in suburban Houston befriends an old man she finds standing naked beside a Dumpster. His problem: He occasionally turns into a fourteen-foot python. 'I am just a very old man who is sometimes a python,' the man tells the woman. 'But you, my child, are a creature far more complex.' One might suspect that Kupersmith, who is working on her first novel, is that creature."

—*Elle*

"The stories shimmer with life. . . . Kupersmith [is] one to watch."

—*Publishers Weekly* (starred review)

"Each of the stories is replete with characters both fabulous and ordinary, stories out of this world and firmly rooted in it. Each is meticulously told by a storyteller talented and wise beyond her years."

—Shelf Awareness

"[A] compelling brand of magic realism . . . enthralling stories . . . *The Frangipani Hotel* is a collection teeming with detail and personality."

—*Asian Review of Books*

"Violet Kupersmith writes about both the old world and the new world with an understanding beyond her years. These stories weave beautifully together to give us a rich tapestry of human history, and present an exciting new voice."

—YIYUN LI, author of *Kinder Than Solitude*

"In this impressive debut, Violet Kupersmith displays a remarkable gift for voice and setting. Using history and horror, mystery and imagination, she has created this vivid collection of haunted and haunting stories. Highly recommended."

—KAREN JOY FOWLER, author of *The Jane Austen Book Club*

"Kupersmith is more than a powerful writer: She's already been admitted into the secret circle of Isak Dinesen and Isaak Babel and Sylvia Townsend Warner. She's a true storyteller, and a demon herself."   —GEORGE DAWES GREEN, founder of The Moth and author of *Ravens*

"Everyone will talk about how young Violet Kupersmith is, how mature and talented beyond her years, but reading these stories of ghosts both ancestral and infernal, you'll become convinced Kupersmith herself is of the spirit world—transcending time, nationality, gender, and place. Rarely does a writer of any age conjure a book so deftly funny and yet so deadly serious—read it, remember it, and then breathlessly await her next one."

—SHERI HOLMAN, author of *The Dress Lodger*

"The haunted world of *The Frangipani Hotel* teems with sensuous and exuberant life. Terror and wonder walk hand in hand. There are ghosts in the air (and in the lake), but there's nothing insubstantial about them. Whether they issue from the war-torn past, the insatiable appetite of nature, or the sinister terrain of the human unconscious is anybody's guess. One thing is certain: They're not going away until the reader too is entirely entranced and captivated."

—VALERIE MARTIN, author of *The Ghost of the* Mary Celeste

THE
FRANGIPANI
HOTEL

THE FRANGIPANI HOTEL

—

Stories

—

Violet
Kupersmith

SPIEGEL & GRAU
TRADE PAPERBACKS

New York

2015 Spiegel & Grau Trade Paperback Edition

Copyright © 2014 by Violet Kupersmith

Published in the United States by Spiegel & Grau, an imprint of Random House, a division of Random House LLC, a Penguin Random House Company, New York.

SPIEGEL & GRAU and the HOUSE colophon are registered trademarks of Random House LLC.

Originally published in hardcover in the United States by Spiegel & Grau, an imprint of Random House, a division of Random House LLC, in 2014.

LIBRARY OF CONGRESS CATALOGING-IN-PUBLICATION DATA

Kupersmith, Violet.
[Short stories. Selections]
The Frangipani Hotel/ Violet Kupersmith
p.   cm
ISBN 978-0-8129-8347-0
eBook ISBN 978-0-679-64514-6
I. Title.
PS3611.U639F73
2013813'.6—dc23   2013013169

Printed in the United States of America on acid-free paper

www.spiegelandgrau.com

2 4 6 8 9 7 5 3 1

Book design by Barbara M. Bachman

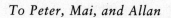

To Peter, Mai, and Allan

CONTENTS

Boat Story · 3

The Frangipani Hotel · 11

Skin and Bones · 53

Little Brother · 77

The Red Veil · 97

Guests · 129

Turning Back · 169

One-Finger · 207

Descending Dragon · 233

Acknowledgments · 243

THE

FRANGIPANI

HOTEL

BOAT STORY

—

"Here, *con*, I cut up a *đu đủ* just for you."

"Oh no, Grandma, I—"

"It's very ripe!"

"Gra—"

"And very good for you too!"

"Grandma! You know I can't eat papaya. It makes my stomach hurt."

"*Tck!* It goes in the trash can then. Such a waste."

"Wait! Why can't you eat it? Or feed it to Grandpa?"

"Grandpa and I are sick of it—we've eaten nothing but *đu đủ* for two straight days because I bought six from that Chinese grocer out in Bellaire last week and now they're starting to go bad."

"Ha! Why did you buy so many?"

"I was hoping for visitors to share them with. But no one

comes to see me. Everyone is too busy—so American! Always working, working, and no time for Grandma. Not even your mother stopped by this week. And the only reason you're here is a silly high school project."

"All right, all right. But I'm only gonna eat a bit, okay? Just this little piece right here. And then we'll do the interview . . . Oh God, it's so slimy . . ."

"Wonderful! Yes, chew, chew—"

"You don't need to tell me to chew!"

"It's disgusting to speak with your mouth full, *con*. Chew, chew. Swallow! See, that wasn't so bad, was it? And it will make your hair shiny and give you good skin. Have another piece."

"My stomach feels weird already, Grandma. But I'll have one more piece while you talk, deal?"

"Oh, making deals now, *hah*? And I thought you weren't sneaky like the other grandchildren. You'll start gambling next. What kind of story did you want me to tell you, *con*?"

"I'm after the big one."

"Oh dear."

"Leaving Vietnam. The boat journey. That's what I want to write about."

"Ask your mother."

"I did, but she was too young when it happened. She only remembers the refugee camp and arriving in Houston."

"Ask your father then."

"He came over on a plane in the eighties, and that's not half as exciting. That'll get me a B if I'm lucky. But your boat person story? *Jackpot.* Communists! Thai pirates! Starvation! *That's* an A-plus story."

"Oh, is that what it is?"

"Mom said you don't like talking about the war, but I should know about my past, shouldn't I? That's what this school project is about—learning your history, exploring your culture, discovering where you came from, that kind of thing."

"You really want to know the country you came from?"

"Yes."

"And you want a story about me on a boat?"

"Yes!"

"Fine. I will tell you a boat story. It begins on a stormy day at sea."

"Wait, wait! Let me get my pencil . . . Okay, go!"

"The waves were vicious, the wind was an animal, and the sky was dung-colored."

"Hang on a second. Where were you?"

"On the boat, of course."

"Well yeah, but is this 1975? We *are* talking about 1975, right?"

"Child, when you're my age you don't bother remembering years."

"But this is at the very end of the war?"

"Did that war ever really end, *con*?"

"Look, Grandma, I just need to get the dates straight! How old were you then?"

"Around the same age as you; I married young. Perhaps a couple years older."

"I think you're getting confused. If Mom was seven when she left, you had to have been way older than sixteen."

"Don't be silly. I remember everything perfectly. This was the day after my wedding. My hair was long and shiny—it was all the *đu đủ* I ate growing up, I'm telling you, *con*—and my teeth weren't bad; they said I could've made a better match than a fisherman. But I did not care about money. Even though we were poor, at the wedding I wore a silk dress embroidered with flowers, and gold earrings that my mother-in-law gave me. After the ceremony I gathered my belongings in a bag and moved onto Grandpa's sampan."

"Okay, we're definitely not on the same page . . ."

"Quiet, *con,* you asked for my boat story, so now listen to me tell it."

"YOUR GRANDPA SPENT OUR first night as husband and wife throwing up the two bottles of rice wine he drank at the wedding reception. In the morning his head was foggy, so he untied the boat and steered us out to sea without paying attention to the signs: the taste of the wind, the shape of the clouds, the strange way the birds were flying. He cast his nets but kept drawing them back empty, and so we drifted farther and farther from land. By the time he noticed how strong the waves were, we could no longer see the shore.

"The storm began, rain drilling down on us as we crouched together beneath a ratty tarp. Our poor sampan bounced on the water like a child's toy. Waves sloshed over the sides, slapping me in the face, the salt burning my nostrils. When our tarp was torn away with a scream of wind, Grandpa and I dug our fingernails into the floorboards of the boat, even though we knew it would do no good in the end.

"*'When we are thrown into the water, cling to my back,'* Grandpa shouted, mostly to hide his fear. *'I will swim us home.'* His breath was still stale with rice wine.

"*But this boat is our home,* I thought. I looked out over the waves that I knew would soon swallow us up. Then to my surprise, I saw a small dark shape bobbing off in the distance. I wiped my eyes and looked again—it was coming toward us. *'Another boat!'* I cried out, overjoyed, thinking we would be rescued after all. Grandpa braced himself against the side of the hull and stood up, waving his arms and yelling as loud as he could. I grabbed on to his feet to keep him from toppling overboard, and together we waited to be saved.

"But as we watched, we realized that the thing approaching us was not a boat after all. I blinked and squinted, not wanting to believe my eyes, hoping that the rain was blurring my vision. Grandpa stopped waving and went silent, his face puzzled at first, then terrified.

"It was a man, not a boat. He was walking upright over the water—I swear it on my mother's dirt grave in Ha Tinh—staggering across the sea as if it was just unruly land. Perhaps I cannot say that it was a man, for it was clear that he was long dead, and from the looks of it had met his end by drowning; the body was bloated and the flesh that hadn't already been eaten by fishes was a terrible greenish-black color. The chest had been torn wide open, and I could see ribbons of kelp threaded among the white bones of its rib cage. Whatever spirit had reanimated the corpse must have been a feeble one, for the body moved clumsily, legs stiff but head dangling loose as it struggled to keep its balance on the angry waves. Grandpa sank down to his knees next to me, and we peered over the gunwale in helpless horror as the body tottered closer and closer.

"When there were only a few feet of churning black ocean left between it and our boat, the corpse stopped. It swayed before us like a drunk man—and for some reason it stood on tiptoe, the decomposing feet arched like a dancer's—dipping and rising with us on each wave but never breaking the skin of the water.

"Grandpa and I waited for the body to move. To talk. To pounce on us. But it simply stood there. I felt it was watching us even though its eye sockets were empty—for the face is where the fish nibble first, you know. We crouched in the boat until our knees hurt, all the while under the sightless gaze of this unnatural thing. Grandpa would have vomited in fright had his stomach not already been empty from throwing up all night. Eventually I couldn't take it anymore; if I was going to die, I wanted to get it over with.

"'*Spirit!*' I called out, my voice so small against the storm. '*What is it that you want?*'

"The drowned man's head flopped down to one side and it turned its rotting palms out to me, as if to show that it didn't know, either.

" 'My husband and I have nothing to give you; no rice or incense to make an offering with. We do not know how to lay you to rest.' A wave slopped over the side of the boat and I received a mouthful of salt water. I spat it out and continued. 'We are just two wet and weary souls, like you.'

"I didn't have to shout these last words, for the wind had begun to quiet down. The rain was no longer beating on my skull and the back of my neck.

"With the jerky movements of a puppet on strings, the corpse lifted its head once more and bent its knees. It had no eyes, no lips or cheeks, and there was only a little bony ridge where the nose had been, yet it still looked sad. Poor thing: lost, half-eaten, and a little too alive to be completely dead. It spun on its tiptoes, then began wandering away across the waves once more. Grandpa thought it went south, and I was sure it went west, though we were probably both wrong, for we were still dazed by the storm. It did not turn to look back at us, and after a while we couldn't see it any longer.

"The waves were far from calm and the sky too dark for us to be optimistic, but Grandpa began steering us toward what we hoped was the shore. When we finally made it back to land we were shaking, but not for the reasons you might think. It wasn't that *thing* we had met out on the water that frightened us, but the fact that we had gotten away so easily. Because what we suspected then was that there would be a price to pay later. I look at it this way: On that stormy day the spirits did not take us, but they wrote our names down in their book, and we knew they would eventually come collecting."

———

"GRANDMA! WHAT THE HELL was that?"

"Watch your mouth, *con.*"

"Seriously, if Mom heard you talking like that, she'd think you were losing it and send you right to an old folks' home!"

"Well, now you know why I never tell your mother any of my stories."

"What am I supposed to do with a story like that? I'm going to fail history! And your papaya is giving me a stomach-ache!"

"*Con,* if you were listening you would have learned almost everything you need to know about your history. The first rule of the country we come from is that it always gives you what you ask for, but never exactly what you want."

"But I want the real story!"

"That was a real story. All of my stories are real."

"No! You know what I mean, I know you do! Why can't you tell me how you escaped?"

"It's simple, child: Did we ever really escape?"

THE FRANGIPANI HOTEL

———

THE ONLY PHOTOGRAPH I have of my father doesn't show his face. He and his two brothers stand with their backs to the camera before their father's grave on a sunny day in April 1973. My grandfather was killed when a building collapsed during the bombings that December, and the incense on top of his tomb—just visible over my uncle's right shoulder—is almost all burned down. All three of the brothers are wearing their traditional silk jackets and trousers, but the trousers are white and don't show up well because of the brightness of the sun and the pale marble of the cemetery all around them. It tricks my eyes whenever I look at it—for a moment I always think they are floating.

The picture hangs in the lobby of the hotel now, on the wall before you reach the stairs, and like everything else in the building, it's covered in a film of perma-grime. My family has owned the Frangipani Hotel on the corner of Hàng Bạc and Hàng Bè since the thirties, when it was *L'Hôtel Frangipane*. Swanky name, shitty place. It's in the Old Quarter, where all the buildings are narrow and crooked and falling apart, and some still have bullet holes from the sixties in their concrete sides. There's a karaoke bar across the street, a massage parlor of ill-repute next door, and the Red River's a couple of blocks east. The Frangi itself is a seven-story death trap, with four-footed things scurrying around inside the walls and tap water that runs brownish. If you slammed a door too hard the entire thing would collapse. It's painted a sickly pale pink on the outside, and lined with peeling brown-and-gold–striped wallpaper on the inside. The large sign that hangs on the front of the whole mess with "The Frangipani Hotel" painted on it is crooked.

When Hanoi was bombed, the building was abandoned and five army officers and their concubines moved in. After the war, when what remained of our family began trickling back into the city, they found maps and diagrams scrawled in chalk on the walls and dusty boxes of ammo stacked in corners. I don't know how they managed to get the place back—the government was still repossessing property and evicting people left and right in the postwar years. Maybe we were lucky. Maybe the place was even too old and nasty for the communists. I don't know how we manage to stay in business now—Hanoi is full of newer hotels in less seamy parts of town, and why anyone would choose to stay at the Frangi instead is one of my favorite diverting mysteries to ponder while I'm working at this shithole.

I'm at the reception desk because I'm the only one who

speaks passable English, and my cousins Thang and Loi are doormen or bellhops, depending on the situation. Thang is the good-looking one—high, chiseled cheekbones, long eyelashes, the kind of red-brown skin that looks warm and like it would smell slightly spicy, the kind of smile that makes women weak in the knees. Loi has the face and personality of a toad. However, he can be useful because his ubiquitous presence dissuades our female guests from trying to sleep with Thang, and because he makes even me seem handsome by comparison.

Their father—my uncle Hung—is legally the owner and manager of the hotel. He and my father and their brother Hai ran it together before the war, but then Uncle Hai drowned in an accident that no one ever talks about and my *Ba* went insane and offed himself a few years later, so now it's his. In his mind, Uncle Hung is a major player in what he refers to as the "Hospitality Industry," and not in charge of a half-star hotel. He's even started calling himself "Mr. Henry" in an attempt to better connect with the Western guests. However, he can't really pronounce "Henry," let alone "Frangipani," so watching him greet guests and introduce himself is endlessly amusing.

The other day, Mr. Henry decided to assemble the family for what he called a "staff meeting." It consisted of him, Thang and Loi, their mother and her sister, who are the housekeepers, me, my mother, who cooks the complimentary breakfasts, and my grandmother—my *Ba Noi*—who either sits upstairs in her room and raves all day or is dragged downstairs by Mr. Henry and positioned in the lobby with a cup of tea to give the hotel a homey feel.

We gathered in the first-floor room where Thang takes his girls and Loi and I take naps on slow days.

"Why are we here? What are we doing here?" Ba Noi said as she sat down.

"I agree," said my auntie Linh. "Why do we need a meeting, Hung? Couldn't whatever it is have waited a couple of hours until dinner?"

"I think Ba Noi is just being generally senile," I chimed in. "She probably doesn't even know we're having a meeting."

Thang and Loi at the same time: "You're a little shit, Phi, you know that? A real shit," and "Don't talk about Ba Noi when she's in the room!"

I looked over at Ba Noi. She was smiling beatifically at a decorative vase of plastic flowers. Mr. Henry—who was wearing only boxer shorts and rubber sandals to his own staff meeting—tried calling everyone to attention. He cleared his throat.

"Valued employees!" he began. He had obviously rehearsed this beforehand. My auntie Mai turned her snort of laughter into a cough when he shot her a look. "Valued employees, I have called this meeting because I have decided that we must change our entire marketing strategy . . ."

I hadn't realized we'd had a strategy, other than not to accidentally poison the guests, or, in Thang's case, accidentally get them pregnant.

". . . We need to add a little more class to our establishment . . ."

Uh-oh. The last time Mr. Henry wanted to add more class to the Frangi, he sank us into debt by installing a heinous plaster tiered-basin fountain in the middle of the lobby that breaks down every month or so.

". . . And we need to reach out to the international corporate community! It's the businessmen from Japan and Australia and Singapore and the USA who have all the money, and so we will convince them to come to the Frangipani Hotel! How will we do this?" Mr. Henry paused dramatically to stare around the room at us. "Easy!" He dragged a large plastic shopping bag from the closet and began to dole out its contents. With his drooping stomach, he looked like a budget Vietnamese Santa Claus. First he pulled out a large stack of looseleaf paper and handed it to Auntie Linh.

"What's this, Hung?"

"Put a little in every room—it's our new, monogrammed hotel stationery! I got it done cheap by a friend on Hàng Ma. Now, for the boys, something special . . ." He reached into the bag again, and as our eyes widened in horror, he slowly drew out two pairs of matching, mustard-colored trousers and jackets with unraveling gold epaulets and tossed them to Thang and Loi. "New uniforms! There, aren't they smart?" Thang stared at the yellow atrocity, looking as if he might cry.

"Snazzy!" I whispered to him. "Imagine what a lady-killer you'll be in that!"

But Mr. Henry rounded on me next. "Phi, you've got English and a bit of French under your belt, right? Well, there should still be some room left up there," he said as he tapped my forehead with a chubby index finger. He dropped a heavy book in my lap. "You're learning Japanese now."

I looked down at the book's cover. Little cartoon children with purple hair smiled up at me. No way.

"Don't you think there's an easier way to do this?" I pleaded. "Maybe repainting the building a color that isn't pink?"

Mr. Henry pretended he hadn't heard me and added, "One more thing—I'm cutting down on your cigarette breaks. It's a filthy habit, and a customer could come in while you're not there. You're down to four a day now."

I'm still feeling sore about this—I've always taken as many cigarette breaks as I pleased, which is probably giving me a mélange of cancers, but it gets me away from the reception desk. During the day I'll just smoke on the corner curb with Thang, but at night I always go around the block to Hoan Kiem Lake. Nothing gives me greater pleasure than leaning against the splintering red bridge that spans it, flicking my cigarette butts into the filthy green water, and staring at people.

Tourists swarm the place even in low season, dutifully snapping photograph after photograph of the ancient tower in the middle of the lake, and giggling Vietnamese teenagers take pictures of themselves on their cellphones. Around the perimeter, couples wander, holding hands, and groups of old women do tai chi to a cassette player warbling bamboo flute music. It's the most crowded spot in the city, but it's where I go to be alone. The water is smeary with the reflections of yellow, green, and blue lanterns hanging from the trees at its edge. Sometimes kids will sit on the lower branches and try to fish, but everyone knows that there's nothing to catch in Hoan Kiem but empty Coca-Cola cans and used heroin needles. Legend says that centuries ago, a giant turtle lived at the bottom of the lake, and it once gave a magic sword to a general to help him defeat the Chinese invaders. I'm supposed to tell the story to all the tourists who stay at the Frangi.

They say that the lake is the soul of this city. I think they might be right.

MONDAY MORNING—I WAKE UP at six as always. I lie in my bed in room 703 for a few minutes and listen to the noise leaking in from the street: the usual motorbike horns, squawks from today's unlucky batch of chickens on their way to market, the propaganda truck making its daily rounds, blasting messages about uniting for the Fatherland. Sunlight is invading the room and I know that the day will be a hot one. It's time for me to get up.

Having been spared the new uniform, I put on the black trousers and blue oxford that I wear every day. I grab my shoes from the hall and head down the stairs, rapping on Loi's and Thang's doors along the way to wake them up.

In the lobby, something feels different but I can't put my finger on what it is. I go about my morning chores—unlocking the front doors, starting the coffee, dusting the family altar, rearranging the room keys hanging behind my desk. The only guests here now are a pair of elderly Swiss tourists, a Vietnamese family from the South on holiday, a handful of Canadian backpackers, and a honeymooning Malaysian couple. No one new is scheduled to arrive for another week. Tourism is slow this time of year, and the hotel is quiet.

Quiet. That's it. It's too quiet. The trickling-piss sound of the tacky lobby fountain provides the background to daily life at the Frangi, and this morning it's silent. The fountain is bone dry. I go over and examine it more closely: no, not quite dry—some moisture clings to the insides and ledges of the basins, and there are patches of water on the floor around it that I hadn't noticed earlier. The fountain is a piece of junk that never works properly, but this is odd even by its standards. Just then Loi comes plodding down the stairs yawning, and I go back to my desk and make a note to call the plumber.

Something else is different, too, but I don't see it until the end of the day when I'm heading upstairs to go to bed: The dust on the glass covering the photograph of my father has been clumsily smeared away in streaks, as if by a large, wet hand.

MR. HENRY'S NEW STATIONERY must be working, because on Wednesday morning an enormous American man arrives unexpectedly, looking for a room. He is rolling a dark green suitcase behind him and carries a black jacket over his arm that is ridiculous in this heat. He says he's in Vietnam for a few days on business and I half-listen as he starts to tell me about his company. His white shirt is translucent in big patches from his sweat. After I check his passport, tell him our rates for day trips to Ha Long Bay, and hand him his key to 502, he lingers by my desk. I see him squinting at the name tag pinned to my chest.

"*Fie?*" he eventually tries.

"It's actually pronounced: '*Fee.*'" Like what you will be forced to pay me when you finally leave, I am tempted to add. Instead, I say, "If you need anything at all during your stay, please don't hesitate to ask."

"Will do, buddy," he says with a grin, and lets Thang take his suitcase and lead the way up the stairs to the fifth floor.

An hour later, a glossy black car pulls up in front of the curb, completely blocking the street. All the neighbors pretend to have something to do outside so they can stare at it. The massage parlor girls from next door look particularly interested. Ten minutes pass and the American descends the stairs wearing a new white shirt, gives me a hundred-watt smile on his way out, and slips into the back of the car, which glides off toward the main street.

I watch through the glass doors as the spectators gradually return to their shops and houses, and then it's time for me to face the ledgers. Wednesday means bookkeeping. It's something I'm good at; I'd rather deal with numbers than people. But today, the longer I look at the figures, the less sense they make. My head aches. The numbers are swimming. I let my head fall and hit the desk a little harder than I anticipated. I raise it again: Mr. Henry is nowhere to be seen, and Thang, resplendent in his urine-colored uniform, is admiring his reflection in the doors while he washes them.

"Take over reception for a little bit," I say to him, and sneak into the first-floor room for a quick nap. The air-conditioning is broken again, but I fall asleep and a minute later I'm dreaming. Dreaming about soup. My Ba Noi and I are sitting on the red plastic stools at the *phở* stall down the street with big steaming bowls of the stuff on the table between us. I stir the soup with my chopsticks and she blows on hers to cool it off. But she blows too hard and bits of broth splash my face. The droplets should be scalding, but they are cool instead.

"Hey. Stop that," I say. But she just laughs and blows on her bowl again so that the *phở* splashes me more. Stop that! Splash. Stop that! Splash. I mean it! Splash.

I OPEN MY EYES and look up at the ceiling. A dark, wet patch is blossoming above my head, and fat drops of water are falling rhythmically on my face. My head is still cloudy from sleep, and for several long seconds I stare up from the bed and blink. Then the switch in my brain flicks on and I leap out of bed as if electrocuted. Fuck. A leak. I jam my feet into my shoes and sprint out of the room.

"Who's staying in two-oh-five?" I call over to Thang. He shrugs. Useless. I sprint to the second floor, my untied shoelaces slapping each step. When I reach the door of room 205 I knock once, politely, then again, more urgently. No one answers. I pound harder. Still nothing. I press my ear against the door and hear the sound of running water from inside. I take a deep breath and push the door open.

I exhale. The bedroom is empty. But a puddle is spreading silently from underneath the bathroom door. Did the toilet break down? Will there be shit all over the place? Could they have drowned? On purpose? A few years after my father did himself in we had another man try to kill himself on the fourth floor, but he ended up fine and it didn't make nearly as much of a mess as this. Oh God, what if they're naked in there?

But when I open the door, the woman I find lying in the overflowing bathtub is fully clothed. She even has her shoes on—delicate black sandals with pointed heels. She is wearing a black *ao dai* embroidered with silver, her eyes are closed, and she rests her head above the water in the crook of her elbow. I'm certain that I've never seen her before. She is young—her skin is pale and smooth, save for a little vertical line between her arched brows—and achingly lovely. You don't get girls like this in Hanoi anymore. She remains perfectly still while the flaps of her dress move like seaweed in the tub. I lean in, gaping, dumbstruck, wondering whether she's alive or dead when she unexpectedly pokes a little pink tongue out and laps at the surface of the water.

I recoil and emit a croaking noise that I hadn't known I was capable of making. It's strange how this small movement startles me more than finding her in the tub in the first place. The girl's eyes snap open, and they are a liquid black.

"I'm sorry," she murmurs, raising her head half an inch. "I

was so very thirsty, and I was too tired to reach the faucet. After I turned the water on I couldn't seem to lift my arms again. Do you think you could carry me?" She rests her head back on the edge of the streaming tub and closes her eyes.

I just stand there, my still-untied shoes filling with water. She opens her left eye. "Please?" she adds, then closes it again.

I roll up my shirtsleeves—I'm not sure why; I end up soaked anyway—and fish her out awkwardly, placing my arms around her back and under her knees. The water gives me goose bumps. Even sopping wet she barely weighs anything. From the size of the puddle she must have been in the tub for almost an hour, yet I notice that she isn't shivering and her fingers and toes remain unwrinkled. I carry her out into the main room and plop her down on the bed because there's nowhere else to put her, and then I slosh back in and turn off the faucet. The bathroom has become a lake that rivals Hoan Kiem; I wouldn't be surprised to look down and find the giant turtle swimming around my ankles. I'm dead, really dead. Mr. Henry is going to flay me, tan my hide, and then mount it in the lobby as a wall decoration.

I sprint out to the cleaning closet at the end of the hall and get a mop and bucket. When I return to the room, the girl has propped herself up slightly on one elbow and pulled the curtain aside to look out the window.

"Where is the tree?" she asks without turning to look at me.

"What?"

She swivels her head to look at me over her shoulder. "You know. The tree. The name. Frangipani." She rolls the English word around on her tongue before returning to Vietnamese.

"*Cây hoa sứ,*" she says and sighs. "You could have reached out and plucked the flowers from this very room."

There are a number of things I want to ask this girl, but all I say, stupidly, is "There is no tree." The line between her eyebrows deepens.

"Oh?" she eventually says after a long moment, then falls silent again and turns back toward the window. When it becomes clear that she has nothing left to say to me, I begin mopping furiously.

"There may be a surcharge," I call out from the bathroom after a while. "For the damages."

"Damages?" There is a note of amusement in her voice. "Of course. Everything will be repaid." It's a strange way to phrase things, but it reassures me. When I have more or less finished cleaning up, I return to the main room. She hasn't moved from her spot on the bed by the window. How do you address a beautiful, potentially unbalanced hotel guest who has flooded your bathroom?

"Miss?"

"Mmm?"

"Miss, I couldn't help noticing that, well, you don't appear to have any luggage with you—no toiletries or bags or anything. Now, I'm not sure how long you've been here, or how long you'll be staying, because I can't remember checking you in, but—"

"It was your uncle who let me in," she interrupts.

Odd that he didn't mention it—we rarely get female Vietnamese guests traveling by themselves.

"Mr. Henry checked you in?"

"What a strange name. Is your name strange, too?"

"Phi. My name is Phi."

"Phi. Would you do me a favor, Phi, and not mention my accident to anybody? I'm rather embarrassed by it. No one saw, and no one really needs to know, do they?"

I stammer out some sort of agreement and she turns and beams at me. Her eyes as they look at me are so dark they appear pupil-less.

"That is so good of you. So very good. But I'm afraid I'm feeling thirsty again. Would you do me another favor and bring me a glass of water from the bathroom?" She slowly lies back in the bed and lets her long black hair fan around her.

"Of course. But let me get you bottled water from downstairs—you shouldn't drink the tap water here; it'll probably kill you."

"Are you sure it won't make me live forever?"

I can't tell if she's making a joke or not, so I smile uncomfortably and shuffle out of the room. I decide to hang the "Do Not Disturb" sign on the doorknob outside; I don't want Auntie Linh or Auntie Mai coming in to clean later and seeing the aftermath of the flood. I also don't want them talking to the girl I found in the tub. The idea of it bothers me for some reason.

When I return to the lobby, I discover that Thang has foisted reception duty on Loi, who is in a panic, trying to give directions in his pidgin English to the elderly Swiss couple from the third floor. As I swoop in to sort things out, my head finally feels clear again. Whatever happened in room 205 seems like a dream.

I pour out a glass of water from the clean jug on the desk, but I don't bring it upstairs. I avoid looking at it for the rest of the day.

The hours pass productively: I get my bookkeeping done, I make small talk with guests on their way in or out and snark about them once they leave, I take my four smoke breaks. The American returns from whatever important business he was on and gives me an overeager, toothy smile. I even decide to crack open my Beginner's Japanese Textbook. *Banzai!*

But I don't touch the glass of water.

On my way to bed, I pause in the stairwell by the second floor. There are footsteps from the hall and I back up against the banister, my heartbeat quickening—I will tell her I'm sorry, I will tell her I didn't mean to forget the water.

But it is Mr. Henry who rounds the corner, not the girl in the bath, and he looks at me quizzically when he finds me lurking on the stairs.

"What are you doing?"

A good question. I'm not really sure myself. The words that come out of me next feel clumsy on my lips, as if they're not mine: "Uncle, I have a question. Was there ever a tree out front?"

"A tree?" He is taken aback. "Yes, there was a tree, a big cây hoa sứ. White and yellow flowers that shed everywhere.

Your father and I had to sweep them up every morning. But that was long before you were born, maybe forty years ago. It was cut down during the war. Now, since you're still up, go and finish the rounds for me and make sure the kitchen and the door to the roof are locked."

IN THE MIDDLE of the night there is a thunderstorm, one of those sudden, violent, lashing storms you get this time of year that come out of nowhere, drench the world, then end as quickly as they started. Lightning silhouettes the crooked Hanoi rooftops and I drift in and out of sleep while the rain throws itself against my window.

But Thursday is so sunny you wouldn't believe a storm even happened were it not for the nasty humidity. It creeps into the hotel from outside, making my collar go limp. Today I'm trying my hardest to be *perky*. Mr. Henry has been giving me odd looks since our conversation on the stairs last night, and I just want things to be normal again. I try whistling as I go about the morning tasks, and even smile at the American when he passes through the lobby on his way to the big black car waiting on the street again.

But everything feels unpleasantly moist, and my headache is back with a vengeance by the afternoon. Thang and I each take a cigarette and go outside. We squat down on the curb and immediately start sweating. It's so hot that the smoke I'm inhaling feels cooler than the air.

Thang is always excessively careful about how he extinguishes his cigarettes, painstakingly grinding them into the sidewalk or even looking for a puddle in the street to actually douse them. Loi, on the other hand, flings his cigarette butts to the ground with violent, spastic movements. Once he accidentally threw one backward and it hit me in the face, an inch below my right eye. Now I only take smoke breaks with Thang.

My cousin takes a drag, then exhales and speaks out of the corner of his mouth.

"I forgot to tell you—the room's free," he says.

"What?"

"The room you were asking me about yesterday when you went crazy and ran up the stairs—two-oh-five. I checked the book and it's free. No one's staying in it now."

It is at that moment that the first potted plant falls from above and smashes on the sidewalk at my feet. A second one follows shortly afterward and lands to my left in an explosion of terra-cotta, clods of dirt, and the remains of a hibiscus. I immediately recognize the blue-glaze phoenix design on the shards of the first pot—it's from my mother's rooftop garden.

"Oh shit, man! Shit! Get inside quick!" Thang hollers at me while he remains on the curb, slowly stubbing out his cigarette. He narrowly avoids being hit by a third potted plant. I grab him by a yellow khaki sleeve and drag him up the front steps and into the lobby.

"Shit, shit," he says, looking outside over his shoulder. "It's like 1972 again. Shit, man, what *was* that?"

I don't answer him because I am taking the stairs two at a

time. When I reach the end of the seventh-floor hallway, I am startled to find the hatch to the roof still closed, latched from my side. I take out my key ring and unlock it, climb the short ladder, and step out, blinking in the sunlight, onto the terrace.

The roof is the only beautiful part of the Frangi, and the part that no one really sees. Over the years my mother has turned the space into a miniature botanical garden, filling it with pots of flowers, dwarf palms, lime trees, hot pepper plants, cacti, and cooking herbs: basil and mint, cilantro and sweet lemongrass. Before he died, my father built a crooked little arbor up here, and my mother has come to sit under it every evening of these two decades since his suicide. I help her and Ba Noi with the watering, and sometimes Mr. Henry does his early morning tai chi up here.

She is curled on her side on the red tiles at the far end of the roof, facing away from me, and still wearing the same ao dai, which looks more silver than black in the sun. As I watch, she slowly extends one sandal-shod foot and nudges a bamboo plant in an elephant-shaped ceramic jar off the ledge. A second later I hear the distant crash, followed by a bellowing that must come from Mr. Henry. The foot is moving dangerously toward a bonsai, and I rush over to try to intercept it.

I am too late. It topples and meets an unfortunate end on the sidewalk below.

"Stop it! Stop!" I skid to a halt precariously close to the unrailed edge and stand over her.

She rolls onto her back to gaze up at me, and her voice when she speaks is too cheerful, too high and strained. It's kind of scary. "It took you long enough to get here," she chirps. Her lips are chapped and her eyes are wild and red-rimmed. For a moment I wonder if she will try to push me off the roof, too.

"I couldn't think of any other way to get your attention," she continues brightly. "I was thirsty, so thirsty, and you never came back! The window was open last night and the rain started coming in, so I just . . ." She pauses and runs her tongue over her lips. "And it tasted so good. It made me stronger, much stronger than your bathwater did. I came up here and drank and drank and drank the rain. But then it ended and the sun was so hot. It made me weak again. I didn't mean to break so many of them, but I was trapped, you see?"

Her lower lip sticks out sulkily. She looks so young; little more than a child. The sun is beating down on the back of my neck and I feel droplets of sweat forming on my temples.

"How did you get up here?" I say quietly. "The only way is through the hatch back there, and it was still closed when I came out. I locked it myself last night."

"Do you really want to know?"

Something drops in my stomach.

"Tell me."

"I crawled out the window and then up the side of the building."

The nonchalance with which she says this makes my skin prickle: Our building has no ladder or fire escape. I look into those dark, dark eyes and there is no doubt in my mind about what she means. Last night, while I was sleeping, she—if I can still call her a she—must have passed by my window as she scaled the slippery concrete, opening her mouth to catch the falling raindrops while she climbed.

"What are you?"

"Oh, Phi, not that question. Ask me anything but that. You don't want the real answer, believe me." She smiles in a way that shows too many teeth.

"All right, how old are you then?"

To my surprise she gives a light, rippling laugh.

"How very cheeky of you, Phi! How very cheeky and how very clever. I'll tell you this much, for I am tired of this game: I'm a great deal older than you think. I can remember many, many things. I remember a time when you could still watch the Chinese junks sailing down the Red River. I remember a man who spoke in French, smelled of opium, and liked to weave the yellow flowers that fell from a certain tree into my hair. I remember the sound of the B-52s, and I remember the rubble. But those memories are hazy. I can remember other things very clearly, Phi, things that might interest you." She pauses and looks up at me with her black eyes. "For example, I can remember things about your father. I can remember him very, very well, and I have an idea that can give both of us what we want." Her voice drops to a low hiss and I have to lean in to hear her next words. "Make me a promise, Phi— promise not to ask me any more questions. If you promise not to ask me any more questions, then I'll promise not to make any more messes. And I'll even tell you something about your father. A secret."

In the back of my mind something is panicking, screaming that this is a bad idea, a very, very bad idea. But I know I will say yes. She knows I will say yes. She has known all along.

"All right."

"Do you *promise*?"

"I promise."

"No more questions?"

"No more questions."

She flashes her feral little smile, and when she speaks again her voice is disturbingly cheerful.

"Good. But I take my promises very seriously, you know. Perhaps I should have told you that before we made our deal. Now, would you carry me back down to my room? Pushing over all those plants has made me very tired. No one will see us—they're all outside cleaning up the mess. And then you can make sure that I have some water to drink, for I'm still thirsty. So very, very thirsty."

Somehow, she seems heavier this time, and I am wheezing when I reach room 205. I set her down on the bed and then I wordlessly dump out the plastic flowers in the large vase on the bedside table, fill the vase from the bathroom sink, and bring it back to her. She takes the vase in her arms and curls herself around it in the bed. Slowly, she dips an index finger inside, daintily swirls it around in the water, then brings it to her lips.

"Thank you, Phi. I'm afraid I'm going to have to ask you not to talk about my little mishap with the plants. If they're curious downstairs I'm sure you'll be able to think of something. Now if you don't mind, I think I need to rest a little— I'm feeling weak after my exertions and it's important that I save my strength. You will see me soon." With that, she closes her eyes, still holding the vase tightly. On my way out I make sure that the "Do Not Disturb" sign is still hanging on the doorknob.

MR. HENRY IS WAITING for an explanation at the foot of the stairs. *I'm so sorry, Mr. Henry, the centuries-old humanoid creature currently napping in room 205 asked me not to talk about it.* I frantically try to think up a story, but nothing's coming. My brain feels waterlogged. When I reach the bottom I still have no idea what to tell him. Possessed by some strange instinct, I ignore him and keep going, walking past him and across the lobby, and then sit down behind my desk and shuffle my papers as if everything were perfectly normal. He comes over and stands in front of the desk, glowering at me. I look up.

"Hello!" I say sweetly, as if addressing a jet-lagged guest.

"Well, what was it?"

"I'm sorry, what was what?" I offer him my most endearing smile.

"The hell is wrong with you, boy? What was happening on the roof?"

"I'm afraid I don't understand. Do you mean . . . what happened on the roof?"

"Of course that's what I mean, you idiot!" He is breathing heavily, as if he has just ingested a particularly strong chili pepper. "Things were falling off the roof. You went up—to the roof—to check on it. What did you see?"

I try a different tactic: "Uh . . . ask me anything but that. You don't want the real answer, believe me." It had worked on me, after all.

Mr. Henry looks as if he might reach across the desk and strangle me, but at that very moment the American providentially returns.

"Gentlemen!" he exclaims as he flings open the glass doors and strides in. The shiny black car is nowhere in sight and his shirtsleeves are rolled to the elbow. He comes right up to the reception desk and pounds a meaty fist on the scratched wood surface. "I have some great news!" he says. Mr. Henry momentarily forgets about the roof and looks over at me expectantly for a translation.

"He has good news."

"Well, why is he telling *me*?" Mr. Henry mutters.

The American is speaking quickly now, and in his excitement a tricky little accent has emerged that I hadn't noticed before. I can barely follow him, let alone translate for Mr. Henry. "I don't know how I did it, but I did it!" I can grasp that. "The big deal I came here for! I'm gonna spare you the details, but it's big, it's real big! We were in the boardroom for six hours today, sweating like pigs the whole time, but the contract got signed in the end." He pumps his fist in the air and gives an honest-to-God "Whoop!" that echoes around the lobby. "New Hanoi branch'll be opening in two months, and the president will be none other than yours truly! How 'bout that? I'm on cloud nine right now; hell, I feel like I could do anything, anything!"

He pauses and looks uncharacteristically shy for a moment before continuing. "Why don't you both come out for a quick drink with me to celebrate? It'll be my treat. I found a great little place, not too far from here." On any other day I would rather re-grout every bathroom in the hotel than go out drinking with the American, but I seize this opportunity to escape from explaining the events of the afternoon.

"We'd love to!" I say to him in English. I turn to Mr. Henry and give him a rough recap in Vietnamese, and then I bolt for the door.

Mr. Henry and I look ridiculous walking behind the American, as if we are the tourists and he is our Hanoi guide. Everyone on the street stares at us as we pass, and some snigger. It doesn't help that we are both a good foot shorter than he is and have to jog awkwardly to keep up with his stride. I've never been this uncomfortable before, which is pretty remarkable considering the past two days. He keeps talking as we walk, and when I feel like it I translate for Mr. Henry, who is more confused than angry now.

"I'm so glad I decided to stay at the Frangipani Hotel instead of the Sofitel," he says. "My company booked me a room there, but there was no local color! No culture! So I decided to walk around the streets and look for somewhere myself—I try not to use the company car unless I have to—and when I saw your place, I said to myself: 'This is it! This is what you've been looking for! This is the real deal!'

"Aah, now we're getting close to it," he says as we round a corner and go down a dank little alleyway. I'm surprised he wasn't mugged the last time he was here. "You know, the guys I work with like to drink at the Royal Club and the Metropole and the expat bars in the French Quarter, but they're missing out, you know? They don't get any of the real Vietnamese experience."

The alleyway ends in a small *bia hoi* joint. There are hundreds of beer stalls like this one tucked into grimy nooks all over the city. I've brought my business to this particular bia hoi before, carousing with Loi and Thang, and it's the same every time: hard white lights, harder plastic chairs, and dirty pitchers of cheaply brewed lager with flies buzzing around the brim. Whenever you're here you try to get as drunk as humanly possible in order to ignore the smells from the slaughterhouse next door. Now, as twilight is falling, half the tables are filled—there are a few olive-uniformed policemen fresh from their shifts, shirtless boys who look too young to be here, and the usual neighborhood drunks—and they all turn and look at us with glassy eyes as we enter.

"Isn't this great?" the American gushes, pulling out Mr. Henry's chair for him. "Yesterday I had the car drop me off in a different part of town so I could try and find my own way around—get a local's feel of *Hanoi*"—the nasally way he pronounces it makes my toes curl—"you know? And on my way back I just stumbled across the place!" By now the proprietor has made his way over to our table with a pitcher of beer and three glasses, which he sets down with wary looks back and forth between the American and Mr. Henry and me. "It's such a shame," the American continues; "most visitors stay on the same, beaten path. They miss discovering the real culture here, and you have such a beautiful, beautiful culture!" He raises his glass in toast to the proprietor—who has retreated back behind his bar and doesn't raise his own glass in return—and then knocks it back. There are snickers from around the room.

To assuage the awkwardness of the situation, and because I have told him that the drinks are on the American, Mr. Henry has picked up a mug of beer in each hand and is swilling from both at record speed.

I pick a drowned fly out of my own beer and try to make myself as inconspicuous as possible. But then I realize that the American is watching me, so I take a sip and try not to grimace. The beer is always warm and tastes like it was distilled inside a cement mixer. But the beauty of it is, the more you drink, the less you taste it. I bring the glass to my lips again.

"That's right! Drink up, buddy!" the American says with his gigantic grin stretched taut across his face. I don't know how he can smile and speak at the same time. I take another swallow and then, with a private chuckle, say:

"I'm very thirsty."

Over the next hour and a half, the American and I don't have to speak much. We are too busy drinking our way through almost three pitchers and polishing off a large platter of fried octopus, which I ordered to test his dedication to the "Real Vietnamese Experience." Even I don't like the stuff. But he gamely gulps down his serving of tentacles, clumsily wielding his chopsticks and taking slurps of beer in between bites.

"Maybe it's just the alcohol," I say in Vietnamese, "but I think the American is growing on me."

Mr. Henry just grunts.

I look over at him; his eyes are unfocused and his face is red. Bright red. Communist-flag-red. "How much have you had, Uncle?" I should have been watching him.

Mr. Henry grunts again, drains his glass, and brings it down to the table with a terrific bang that makes the rest of the patrons of the bia hoi jump.

"Look at me," he slurs in Vietnamese. "Old. Done. What a wasted life I've led! You and the foreign one . . ." Mr. Henry points a little to the left of the American, blinks, then corrects himself. "You don't understand because you're both still young. But just you wait!"

I've seen Mr. Henry smashed enough times to know that he has reached the monologue stage of drunkenness, which precedes his passing out. The American, who doesn't understand a word, smiles pleasantly and nods his head. Everyone in the joint hushes their conversation to listen in on our table.

"Uncle," I say as I carefully slide the pitcher of beer away from him, "maybe it's time to go home now—"

"Don't interrupt your elders, boy! What was I saying? No one ever appreciates me: I wake up every morning with pains in my back, but I'm the only one keeping the goddamn hotel running! My own mother's a cockroach, eating me out of house and home and too old and mean to die. My sons have one working brain between them. You're a little wise-ass who smokes too much. But it's the women who're the worst—Linh, Mai, and your mother—there's never any rest from it, the nagging, nagging, nagging. Ask him if he's married," he says to me, indicating the American.

I do, and the American holds up his left hand in response. A gold ring on his thick fourth finger glints underneath the bia hoi lights. "To the most wonderful woman in the whole wide world," he says. Gag. I translate for Mr. Henry and he laughs.

"Let me tell you something about women. Translate for me, Phi. Did you know that in Hanoi, they say the most beautiful girls live in Saigon? In Saigon, they say the most beautiful girls live in Hue. In stuck-up Hue, they say that Saigon is right. But everyone is wrong: There are no beautiful girls left. Pretty faces, sure. But then they ring their eyes with all that dark makeup. They wear see-through blouses and run around in packs, shrieking and squealing and always fiddling with their cellphones and their dyed hair." His voice breaks off, and when he speaks again there is a note in it that I've never heard before. "Whatever happened to the simple girls, the sweet girls, the girls that you could sing about? All my life, I've only ever known one girl like that."

I don't translate the last bit. "Who, Auntie Linh?"

He snorts. "Of course not. It was a girl who stayed in the hotel once, a long time ago, passing through, from—oh, I can't remember anymore. But she stole all our hearts in the week she was here. I was a bit younger than you then, weedy and small, and she only had eyes for Hai and your father. This was before your mother was in the picture, by the way," he adds, because he can tell that I am trying to calculate the dates in my head. "And before your father started to go . . ." He makes a waggly finger gesture by his temple. "Well, you know. I think they both believed that they could get her to stay somehow, and marry one of them. That's how besotted they were—we were—with her."

The American has been quietly drinking his beer this whole time. Though he can't understand, his smile has faded slightly and his eyes flicker back and forth between the two of us over his glass. But I can't worry about him right now; Mr. Henry has been gradually tilting forward over the course of his little speech, and by now he is slumped over the table, barely holding himself up on his elbows. *Don't pass out yet, Mr. Henry,* I think to myself. *Hold out just a little bit longer.* I am acutely aware of my own heartbeat. "What happened?" I ask softly.

He gives a hollow little laugh. "What happened? You already know what happened. Of my brothers, I was the luckiest," he says, and then his face hits the table.

For a moment everything is frozen. Then Mr. Henry snores loudly. The world clicks back into place and I remember where I am, and that the American is still sitting across the table from me.

An awkward silence, punctuated by Mr. Henry's periodic snoring, ensues. I register the American picking up the pitcher and reaching over the mass of Mr. Henry to refill my glass. More silence. Then he clears his throat and says, out of nowhere, "Your English is really good, did you know that?"

I snap my eyes up from staring at my unconscious uncle. *Of course I know how good my own English is,* I think, my lip automatically lifting to sneer. Then I realize what I'm doing and want to laugh. I don't know why, but Mr. Henry's story has me rattled, and now I'm grateful to the American for saying something irrelevant, something innocuous. For breaking the spell. My cheeks are warm, so I know that I am approaching drunk, but I've still retained my pandering ability and reply, "Do you really think so? I'm flattered. In school it was the only class I liked. But I get so embarrassed about my accent."

The American gives me what he probably thinks is a gentle, friendly punch in the shoulder with his gigantic fist. "Aww, Phi, don't even—your accent is great. Your English is great, really great. In fact . . ." He breaks off to drain the rest of his glass, wipes his mouth on the back of a huge pink hand, and leans toward me over the table. The alcohol on his breath is overpowering. "In fact, I want to make you a proposition, Phi. I know this is a bit sudden, but don't think I'm just saying this because I'm drunk—and I *am* drunk—but that, that's beside the point, and the point is that I could use a guy like you. I know I'm rushing this—I fly home to the States on Saturday morning—but I'm coming back to Hanoi in six weeks, and then things will start moving fast. We need people like you: sharp, hardworking. People with your language skills. People who know the way this city works. To be advisers and go-betweens, to do PR. I know it's kind of unusual, to be doing things this way, but I think it's a sign that I met you by chance. You're young, you're clever, you can do whatever you want to!"

I don't have the energy to be surprised by anything anymore. Even the American's spontaneous job offering. "That's very nice of you," I say flatly.

"I'm not saying it to be nice, I'm saying it because it's true. Do you want to end up like him?" He inclines his head toward Mr. Henry, who has a dribble of spit hanging from the corner of his mouth. That's when I start to have dangerous thoughts. *I could do it,* I think. *I could leave. What's keeping me here?*

Slowly, I hold out my hand to him across the table. He reaches out his own and shakes mine, and when I pull away there is a business card pressed against my palm.

"You hold on to that. Phi, you've got my word, I'll be back in six weeks' time, and then we're gonna be running half of this city."

He pours us both refills and we clink our glasses and drink. He looks thoughtful for a moment, then strangely shy. Then he says, "There's one thing in the meantime that I could use your help with." Ah. I've been waiting for the catch. "The thing that he—is he your dad?"

I shake my head. "No. Uncle."

"The thing that your uncle was talking about before—the beautiful girls of your country. I thought it would be a shame to pass up the chance, since I'm here, in"—he pauses and runs his fingers through his hair—"in Asia. Just for one night. I've been on the road so much lately, and it can get lonely—"

"I think I know what you mean," I break in, so I don't have to hear any more. "I can give you the name of a place in Ba Đình—"

"Wait, hear me out. I don't mean . . . I don't want a whore. I'm not looking to sleep with anybody . . ." The American is offended now. "I just want to take a young, beautiful girl out to dinner, out dancing. I want to put my hand around her waist, to talk to her, to laugh with her. Nothing more. Is that so wrong of me?"

I shrug.

"Look," he says, smiling again, "to show you that my intentions are nothing less than honorable, I'm gonna take you with me." He laughs. "You can be my chaperone. How about tomorrow night? You arrange everything with the girl, and let her know I mean well, that I'm not a creep or anything. We'll all go to dinner at eight. Sound good?"

I've already made too many strange deals today, and I hesitate before this one.

"Okay," I say eventually.

"Great!" He stands up and points at Mr. Henry. "Now let's get this big boy home."

I stand, too, and am alarmed by the way the world wobbles when I do. The American drops an enormous pile of bills on the table without counting them, and we hoist my uncle between us and stagger off down the alleyway. It's mostly the American who's supporting Mr. Henry's weight—I'm struggling enough trying to keep myself upright. Thankfully, the streets are practically deserted by now, and the only person who witnesses our walk home is an old man burning a paper spirit-offering in the gutter.

—

THE AMERICAN AND I deposit Mr. Henry in the first-floor bedroom. On our way up the stairs I turn to him and say, "It feels funny, working together like this, but I guess I should start getting used to it, huh?"

"What?" he says. I realize that I have been speaking in Vietnamese.

I tell him good night in English and leave him at the second-floor landing, saying that I have something to take care of. Without knocking, I throw open the door to room 205. The girl hasn't moved from the bed, but the flower vase is now lying empty on its side. I'm a little disappointed—I had been hoping to burst in on her doing something, I don't know what. Maybe hanging upside down from the ceiling. She wrinkles her nose at me.

"You've been drinking, Phi."

"It was the American's fault! He's going to be my new boss. And he wants me to get him a call girl, to not-sleep with her tomorrow night."

"You're drunk, Phi."

"Probably—I'm seeing two of you right now."

She laughs. "Oh, there's only one me; you should be thankful for that."

"Your vase is dry. Let me fill it."

"That's very kind of you, but I'm not thirsty anymore. A little hungry, but not thirsty."

"I'll get you something to eat then."

"That won't be necessary. Not yet, anyway. Now it's time for you to rest. I'll be fine for the time being. Sleep well, Phi."

Feeling rejected, I fumble out the door and feel my way down the hall and up the stairs, pausing by various rooms. I know that 312 has nightmares, I know about the stains that were on 404's sheets this morning. I know things about them that would make them blush, but most of them probably don't know my name. I fall into bed without taking my shoes off. Everything is tilting in a way it shouldn't. It feels a little bit like I'm underwater.

THE NEXT MORNING, Mr. Henry is too hungover to care about the broken plants anymore. He stumbles into the lobby complaining about his aching head, and if he remembers the things he said last night, he does not acknowledge it. My own head, however, feels surprisingly clear. I sit behind my desk and wait for the American to come down the stairs, steeling myself for the inevitable moment to come when he will apologize and tell me that he didn't know what he was doing last night and didn't mean any of it.

A little after nine, the black car pulls up outside, and the American, his hair slicked back and his face pinkish, emerges. As he passes me on the way out, he says, "Hey there, partner. Eight still all right?" with a wink.

I nod, my pulse racing like a flustered schoolgirl's. After he drives away, I pick up the phone and make a call to the massage parlor next door. Thang comes swaggering down the stairs just as I am hanging up the receiver.

"Who was that?" he asks, squeezing in next to me on the chair. He kicks his feet up on top of the desk and steals my mug of coffee from me.

"Just business. I need you to cover reception for me tonight."

"Can't. Got a date. Make Loi do it." He takes a sip of coffee. "This is too sweet."

"I put condensed milk in mine. If you don't like it, get your own."

"It's fine."

We sit together in the chair without speaking. He drinks my coffee and I stare out across the lobby at the wall where the photograph of our fathers hangs. I want to tell him I'm leaving, but when I open my mouth I say, "Who do you think was holding the camera?"

BY 7:45 P.M. I am waiting nervously in the lobby. Loi, the little shit, agreed to take over reception tonight, but he's nowhere to be seen. Neither is Châu—or "Candy," as she's professionally known—from next door, who told me that she specializes in showing Western men a good time while getting them to empty their wallets. I pace around the still-dry fountain; I haven't gotten around to calling the plumber yet. Why does my head hurt now when it felt fine this morning?

At 7:58 the American's black car purrs to a stop in front of the Frangi and he sidles out wearing a crisp black suit. I can tell that my wrinkled blue oxford is a little damp under the armpits and smells like stale beer. I open the door for him, stammering out an excuse for running behind schedule, but he is looking past me, at something over my shoulder. The American gives a low whistle. "You sure know how to pick 'em, Phi."

I turn around. She is standing at the foot of the stairs, her hand resting lightly on the banister. The edges of her black and silver ao dai undulate gently, as if there were a breeze in the lobby, and her hair falls over her shoulders, so dark it almost looks blue.

"Oh no," I say. "This isn't—"

Her high, clear voice cuts me off: "Hello," she says in halting English. "I will be escorting you this evening."

The American shoulders past me and walks over to her with his hand outstretched. "A real pleasure to meet you," he says. When he reaches her, she looks down at his hand with an amused expression but does not shake it. The American recovers, sweeping his arm out and making a funny bow. "What is your name?" he asks her.

With a sudden jolt I realize that it hasn't once occurred to me to ask her this myself. She appears to be giving the matter some consideration. After a pause, she says, "You may call me Tien."

"Well, Miss Tien," the American says, butchering the pronunciation, "shall we?" He starts to offer her his arm, then thinks better of it and makes a flourish in the direction of the door instead. She smiles and walks across the lobby—I've never seen her walk before, and oh, can she walk, swaying slightly, her little heels making no sound on the tile, as if she's drifting above it. Without giving me so much as a glance, she sashays out the door to where the shiny black car is waiting, the American close behind.

For a moment I stand there, stunned, until I hear Loi's clomping footsteps on the stairs. "If Candy from the massage parlor ever shows up, she's all yours!" I call to him, and nip out the door in time to hear the American saying:

"I hope you're hungry!"

And her reply: "You can't even imagine."

The driver is waiting for me with the door open. I duck inside the automobile, running my fingertips over the buttery leather of the seats and inhaling its scent deeply. Then the door closes with a soft click, and we pull away into the sea of motorbike headlights drowning the streets of the city.

TONIGHT, THE AMERICAN HAS abandoned his pursuit of the Real Vietnamese Experience and is clearly trying to impress "Tien" instead. His car delivers us to a restaurant behind the opera house that has no name, just a gold sign above the glass door with the engraved image of a lotus. We enter the foyer and—as I obviously don't belong and will never set foot in the place again—I gawk at the surroundings without shame. Giant orchids line the walls and dangle from wires, while live orange-and-blue butterflies float around the room or rest on the flowers. I look down: Marble tiles gleam beneath the unevenly worn-down heels of my cheap shoes. The dining area is through another glass door, and it is dominated by a cascade of water at the center of the room, which falls from some unseen source in the ceiling into a circular pool in the ground. I hope that Tien isn't in one of her thirsty moods.

The waiter who seats us looks familiar—I'm pretty sure his mother runs a beauty salon on Hàng Quạt. He may be wearing a suit that costs more than the Frangi's yearly electrical bill, but he's still a plebe like me underneath it. Our boy suavely pulls out Tien's chair for her, simpers at the American, and gives me a very special sneer. There is no menu. The American asks for a certain kind of wine, our boy nods, fetches it, pops it, and pours, and then the food just begins arriving—food I've never even dreamed of: a cool, creamy soup, pink slivers of tuna that melt on the tongue, a duck on a bed of dainty greens, oysters still trembling in their shells, a faintly musty cheese . . . the plates keep on coming.

I glance around the room at the other diners and am not surprised to see that it's mostly middle-aged Western businessmen and ambassador-types with younger Vietnamese women. I am the only Viet guy here, apart from the waiters, and the only male in the room without a necktie on. The men are all in black or gray suits and swigging wine liberally. Some of the women are in ao dai, and some wear slinky Western dresses. Their eyebrows are all identically arched, and they pick at their foie gras with their forks in the exact same way. They are nothing compared to Tien.

Tonight she is radiant and she knows it. Tonight she is a thing of jewels and precious metals: gold skin, onyx hair, silvery dress, and eyes like diamonds—shining and hard and cold. I haven't said a word to her all evening because she has been too busy charming the American to let me get anything in edgewise. Tien doesn't even touch her food; she chirps nonstop in the English I didn't know she could speak, spinning endless stories about the history of the city or telling the American to drink more wine. I'm not touching alcohol tonight—not after yesterday. The American is half-drunk already, and laughing at everything Tien says, his gaze never leaving her face. While she chatters and he laughs, I devour my food as if there's no tomorrow. I am perfectly aware that I am wolfing down my meal in a way that is most unbecoming for such an establishment and don't need our boy's continued stare of disapproval to tell me. When I ask him for chopsticks so I can eat even faster, he just glares at me.

Maybe an hour later, I am polishing off the last course— a tart with candied fruit that oozes chocolate—and the American is utterly smitten. While I scrape the plate with my fork, he motions the waiter over and wordlessly hands him a credit card. It's disappointing; I had been hoping to hear the astronomical price of the dinner. Tien dabs at her mouth delicately with a napkin, which seems silly because she hasn't lifted her fork to her mouth all night.

As we pass through the foyer again on the way out, I wonder briefly if the butterflies ever accidentally escape, and whose job it is to chase after them when they do.

———

Outside, the American goes to wave over his car from the corner where it has been waiting, but then Tien surprises both of us by suddenly placing her hand on his arm to stop him.

"Actually," she says sweetly, "I was hoping that we might take a little walk. It's a cool night, and the only way to really know my city is by foot."

The American grins. "What a coincidence! I've always thought the same thing!" he says. He motions for the car to stay put, and Tien lets him place his huge arm around her waist. She looks so fragile next to him. I trail behind them as she starts to lead us in the direction of Hoan Kiem Lake.

It's Friday night and the streets are so crowded that the people—revving their motorbikes, stumbling out of bars in one another's arms, buying and selling things that no one needs—just become noise. There are so many people that I don't even see them anymore. The streets are so crowded that they are empty. No one notices the girl wearing a black and silver dress and a secret smile, the man with stars in his eyes who follows her, or the boy in a dirty shirt behind them both.

We are standing at the southern edge of the lake in the shadow of the willow trees. I look out across the water with its rainbow sheen of oil and feel the light and sound pulsing at its shores.

"It's beautiful," says the American, who has forgotten that I am here.

"It is my home," says Tien.

I say nothing.

"You're beautiful," says the American.

"Is that so?" says Tien.

I still say nothing, but a vague sense of uneasiness is creeping in the back of my mind.

The American, his face so earnest it hurts, turns to her. "Of course you're beautiful!" he exclaims. "You're the most beautiful woman I've ever met. When I'm with you, I feel . . . I feel . . . I can't even describe how I feel. But I would do anything for you."

A slow smile begins to blossom on Tien's face, causing a little spike of fear to run through me. "Do you really mean that?" she says. "Would you really do anything for me?"

"I would. In a heartbeat."

"Do you promise?"

No. No, No.

"I promise."

Tien's smile widens. "Let's test this, then," she murmurs. "Look across the lake, toward the middle. Do you see the old tower there? On the little island near the center? It's not very far away, is it? I bet even an old man could swim to it and then back without any trouble."

The intrepid American is already taking off his jacket: "Well, Miss Tien, I'm gonna do it for you." He steps out of his shoes and lines them up so that the toes are facing the lake. People mill about on the shore, but no one sees and no one cares. As he goes to step into the water I make a move toward him, but Tien sinks her fingernails deep into my forearm and the pain is so sharp it stops me from even making a sound. The American wades out five feet before he turns and calls to Tien over his shoulder.

"Time me," he says, laughing, before pushing off into the darkness with powerful strokes, the moonlight on his back.

The girl and I watch him from the shore. Eventually she extricates her nails from my arm.

"You made me bleed!" I cry.

She either doesn't hear me or pretends not to. "It's a shame," she says cheerfully. "He would have made it, you know." Without taking her eyes from the American in the water, she lifts her fingers to her mouth and licks them off one by one.

"Why won't he?"

She steps delicately into the lake. I jump in after her. It is much shallower than I expected. "Why won't he?" I ask again, more urgently. "Answer me!" Her black and silver dress is turning into moonlit ripples on the water, and her hands are covered in scales. She turns and gives me a triumphant smile, or maybe she is just baring her teeth.

"Oh, Phi," she says. "You've broken your promise."

I stop with my shirt still dry. She slips away until only her head is still visible.

"Why not me?" I whisper to the lake because I have already lost.

"How funny," she says before vanishing beneath the surface. "Your father asked the very same thing!"

And I find myself alone, standing waist-deep in the water.

SKIN AND BONES

———

Mrs. Tran had been considering it for a long time, but she made up her mind for certain when she found her younger daughter Thuy in the kitchen, crouched like an animal in front of the open refrigerator, ripping off chunks of a leftover chocolate cake with her bare hands and devouring it. Calmly, Mrs. Tran took the cake from Thuy's hands, lowered it into the trash can, then went and made one of her rare ten-cents-a-minute calls to Grandma Tran in Vietnam to make the arrangements. That very day she booked both of her girls round-trip tickets—Houston to Ho Chi Minh City, twenty hours with a three-hour layover in Seoul—leaving that very weekend and returning at the end of the summer holidays three weeks later. Thuy and Kieu's father, who lived with his new wife and children in Atlanta, paid for the plane tickets because he owed the girls birthday presents. Mrs. Tran told Thuy and Kieu that the trip was a chance for them to rediscover their roots, but Thuy knew the real reason: Her mother was sending her away in the hope that she would lose fifteen pounds on a diet of fish and rice, maybe even more if she could catch a bug from the street food or dirty ice. Vietnam was Fat Camp.

Kieu complained at first. She wasn't like Thuy—*she* had friends and boys waiting to flirt with her and pool parties to attend in spangled bikinis. Their mother, however, was un-yielding; Thuy couldn't possibly go alone. Mrs. Tran would go herself but she couldn't take all that time off work. Besides, Grandma Tran wanted to see both of her grandchildren—she was getting on in years and wouldn't live forever.

Thuy also suspected that her older sister—the skinny sibling, her mother's accomplice in everything—was being sent along to monitor everything that Thuy ate. Kieu was an obedi-ent calorie snitch, always quick to notice if there were potato chip crumbs on Thuy's shirt or incriminating spoon marks in the tub of ice cream, but she was no match for Thuy, the junk food mastermind. As she packed her suitcase, Thuy planted several decoy chip bags near the top, hidden in an easy place for Kieu to find when she searched it later. Satisfied, her sister would overlook the box of cookies stashed near the under-wear at the bottom, the chocolate bars in the toiletries bag, and the packets of cheesy snacks tucked carefully into each of Thuy's sneakers.

The funny thing was that Kieu had once been the fat one. She had weighed almost ten pounds at birth and spent the first few years of her life as an immense, hairless Buddha of a baby.

Thuy, born two years later and three weeks premature, had been scrawny in comparison. But over the years they had gradually switched places; Thuy ate her way to shapelessness while Kieu emerged from childhood slender as a rice stalk. Their mother didn't bother correcting visitors who saw their baby pictures framed on the wall and automatically mistook Baby Kieu for Baby Thuy. Mrs. Tran, who hovered just shy of five feet and had never weighed over a hundred pounds in her life, often speculated about how she had produced daughters capable of such corpulence. Guiltily, she wondered if Kieu's infant weight and Thuy's current state were her body's deferred response to the weeks in her own youth that she had spent starving, bobbing in a refugee boat on the South China Sea. Perhaps she had genetically tried to provide her offspring with some extra padding should the same fate befall them.

The night before their departure, Mrs. Tran snuck extra Pepto-Bismol tablets, mosquito repellent, and bottles of hand sanitizer into Thuy's and Kieu's backpacks. She gave them a piece of paper listing the addresses and telephone numbers of all their relatives, and another with Vietnamese phrases and their English translations to memorize, which she handed over with a lament that she had not taught them more of their mother tongue. Thuy glanced down at the sheet: "Please help!" "How much does it cost?" "I'm lost!" "Where is the bathroom?" "Call the police!" "Don't touch me!" She gave them some money to give to Grandma Tran, some money to bribe the customs officers, and some money for themselves. Finally, nervously, she gave them a photograph of herself and their father as teenagers, standing in front of the Notre Dame of Saigon, both of them young and smiling and very, very thin. It was the first picture their mother had ever shown them from her old life in Vietnam.

"You should find this exact same spot and take a picture of yourselves there!" Mrs. Tran said. And then she surprised her daughters and herself by bursting into tears on the spot. Both Thuy and Kieu were unsure how to react to this rare display of emotion; Thuy looked down at her hands while Kieu awkwardly patted her mother's arm. "I'm just going to miss you two so much," said Mrs. Tran between snuffles. But somehow Thuy didn't quite believe her.

ON THE AIRPLANE, Kieu had the aisle seat, Thuy had the middle, and an elderly Vietnamese man with a pencil mustache sat by the window.

"Going home?" he said to them in Vietnamese as they adjusted their seat belts, then in English when he realized they didn't understand.

"Just visiting," Kieu replied. Then, she added, "We're going to Vietnam to rediscover our roots."

"I'm going to rediscover my waistline," Thuy muttered under her breath.

She was restless for the entire trip, the thought of the three weeks to come weighing heavy and gelatinous on her heart. The last time they had gone to visit their grandmother had been four years ago, and for only a week. Thuy had been eleven then, approaching chubby but not yet at a weight that alarmed her mother, and Kieu had been thirteen. Their mother came with them on that trip—her first time back in the country since she had left it in a fishing boat in 1975. She and Grandma Tran had spent every day peeling and eating fruit at the kitchen table, exchanging twenty-three years' worth of gossip, while Kieu, who fancied herself a preserver of oral history, sat and listened to them talk even though she had no idea what they were saying. Thuy had just watched poorly dubbed Chinese soap operas in another room. When her mother went back to Vietnam again, two years after the first trip and two years before this one, Thuy and Kieu had stayed home.

It turned out that they didn't need the bribe money to get past customs—the officer was a pimply youth whose olive uniform was too big for him, and he was so distracted by Kieu's low-cut blouse that he barely glanced at their paperwork before stamping it. The two sisters stepped, yawning, into the hot Saigon sunlight, where they waited on a curb for Grandma Tran to pick them up. There was a stall selling hot pork buns nearby—fat, fluffy things the size of a man's fist— and Thuy's mouth began to water.

"Give me some money," she said to Kieu. "I want to buy a *bánh bao*."

"Nope," said Kieu nastily. "You're shaped like a bánh bao already. The last thing you need is to eat more of them."

Grandma Tran was nowhere in sight. The sidewalk was

uncomfortably warm so both girls sat on top of their suitcases. Thuy hoped that her cookies weren't squashed or melted. Kieu fanned herself with her passport. They sat on the side of the road and roasted in the sun for an hour and twenty minutes before deciding to take a taxi.

"WE! GO! HERE!" Kieu told the driver in loud, slow English. She handed him the sheet of paper with the list of relatives written on it in their mother's even script, and pointed to their grandmother's address at the top.

The taxi dropped them off early because the *ngõ* where their grandmother lived was far too narrow and crowded for the car to drive down. Motorbikes clogged the road while skinny kids in cutoff shorts and dusty rubber sandals chased one another through the traffic; a fruit market took up half the street; men perched on plastic stools at every corner, gambling, the outlines of their ribs visible through white undershirts; old women, their flesh hanging from thin bones, emptied pails of foul-smelling liquid into gutters from their doorways.

Thuy and Kieu dragged their suitcases through the fray, stumbling over holes in the pavement and pausing frequently to brush sweaty strands of hair from their eyes. People stopped and watched their labored progress without bothering to hide their amusement. Several young children began to run in circles around the sisters like gnats, dispersing only after one of their mothers yelled something sharply at them from a balcony. After making it only a few blocks, the girls stopped so Thuy could catch her breath and Kieu could look up the house number. It was then that they discovered they had forgotten to get the paper with the address back from the taxi driver. Kieu said that it was Thuy's fault, and Thuy was too hot and tired to disagree. However, they both had a vague idea of where their grandmother lived from their visit four years earlier. Thuy remembered that it was next door to a noodle shop, and Kieu was fairly sure that the building was yellow, with dark shutters. They found it five minutes later when Thuy caught a whiff of noodles and followed the scent to the correct block.

The house was smaller than they recollected; it was flanked by the noodle shop on one side and a modern-looking apartment building on the other, and was dwarfed by both. The shutters were closed, and the dark yellow paint was warped and peeling from the sun and the humidity. When Kieu knocked, the door swung inward almost immediately, but opened no farther than a couple of inches.

"Hello?" said Kieu.

A familiar crinkly face appeared in the space a moment later. "Allo!" Grandma Tran rasped, grinning with a mouth that was missing many of its teeth. She opened the door just wide enough to let the girls and their suitcases in, then closed it again once they were through. Grandma Tran only came up to Thuy's and Kieu's shoulders, so she stood on her tiptoes to give them each a kiss on both cheeks. She did not seem to realize that she had forgotten to pick them up at the airport, but the girls didn't know enough Vietnamese to ask her about it. They removed their shoes—one of the few Asian traditions that they observed back home in Houston—and followed their grandmother down the hallway and into the kitchen, where dark stone tiles cooled the soles of their exhausted feet. The light was dim and vaguely pinkish; since their last visit, the window that looked out to the back garden had become almost completely obscured by a bougainvillea exploding with magenta blossoms.

Thuy noticed the smell as soon as she stepped inside but didn't mention anything until Grandma Tran was busy getting them something to drink from a suspicious-looking pump in the yard. "What *is* that?" she whispered to Kieu.

"What's what?"

"That smell."

"What are you, some kind of bloodhound? I don't smell anything."

Thuy couldn't describe the odor. It was subtle: a bit like the beach at low tide, a bit like the congealed goat's blood stew her mother used to make, a bit like a too-ripe pineapple, and it seemed to emanate from the very walls of the house. It clung heavily to their grandmother, too, as she noticed when Grandma Tran returned bearing two glasses of water that tasted surprisingly clean.

As Thuy sat at the table and sipped her water in silence, the jet lag finally hit her. She found that her eyelids refused to stay open, her body ached from her toenails to the roots of her hair, and her chin kept dropping to her chest when she least expected it.

"You slip?" Grandma Tran asked them sharply, rousing Thuy. Thuy caught Kieu's eye and saw that her sister was just as confused as she was. Their minds both worked at the same time to decipher the accented English: Slip? Sleep!

"YES! YES! WE ARE VE-RY SLEE-PY!" said Kieu in the same voice she had used with the taxi driver. But before Thuy could rest, Kieu insisted on letting their mother know that they had arrived safely. This turned out to be a messy and expensive ordeal involving miming things to their grandmother, three different phone cards, repeated dialing, lots of static, and yelling into the receiver. Grandma Tran didn't even get to speak to her daughter because just as she took the phone from Thuy the line went dead.

The girls, too tired to lift their suitcases, dragged themselves to the spare room upstairs. They sank into the mattress in unison, and promptly fell asleep for sixteen hours. So ended their first day in Vietnam.

It was Kieu, not Thuy, who was ready to pack up and return to America from the start. "I can't stand it!" the older sister said to the younger as they lay in bed on the fifth night. "I have no one to talk to—Grandma doesn't understand English, and you never say anything! It's like living in a house with two ghosts!" When Thuy didn't bother replying, Kieu let out a frustrated little scream, pulled the sheet over her head, and complained to herself under the covers until she fell asleep. Thuy stayed awake for a while longer. She hated sharing a bed with her sister because Kieu had a habit of clinging to things in her sleep, and tended to grab Thuy's belly fat, squeezing the flesh tightly with her bony little fingers all night long. Thuy found it odd that Kieu was so supportive of their mother's war against her expanding waistline, because if Thuy were to actually lose the weight, her sister would have nothing to hold on to.

Thuy didn't mind that she and her grandmother couldn't speak to each other. In fact, she rather liked it, and found that their mutual lack of language skills freed them from the banalities of conversation. They had a routine now: Every morning, she, Kieu, and Grandma Tran took a walk around the neighborhood at a time when, at home, the girls would have still been in bed. They had been reluctant to venture outside since the circus of their arrival, but to Thuy's amazement, no one paid her any heed; no one stared, no one laughed, no one looked at her at all. When she was with her grandmother, she was a local; she was invisible. Grandmother and granddaughters would shuffle down the street, turn right at the fruit market, and then walk until they reached the river, where they would stop to rest. In the soft morning sunlight, with the breeze off the water blowing back her gray hair, Grandma Tran always looked heartbreakingly young. She would clamber up on the lowest rung of the guardrail, her arthritic feet hanging out of the backs of her sandals, and lean over the edge, watching boats make their way toward the sea. At these moments, Thuy always wondered if Grandma Tran was thinking about her daughter in America. If she had known the words, she might have asked.

After a time, the sun would become stronger, causing little

prickles of perspiration to start at the back of Thuy's and Kieu's necks—Grandma Tran, however, never seemed to sweat—and they would make their way back to the house.

Later in the day, when the heat was at its most vicious, a heavy drowsiness would steal over both Kieu and Thuy and they would take cots out on the balcony overlooking the back-yard and nap. During this time, Grandma Tran napped, too, but she always stayed in her overgrown garden. Thuy, through drooping eyelids, could half-see her grandmother stretched out on her favorite patch of grass, her figure hazy in the sun-light, surrounded by lush vegetation and crooked fruit trees. She wasn't sure why, but in these moments between waking and dreaming, the strange smell would become much stronger, assaulting Thuy's senses with its cloying aroma. Each day, it was the last thing she remembered before falling asleep.

But by the time she woke up the smell had always abated, and she and Kieu, rubbing the sleep from their eyes, would go downstairs to the kitchen, where Grandma Tran was waiting with slices of tasteless, pulpy fruit for their afternoon snack. Thuy was almost happy here; she liked spending time with Grandma Tran, she liked being away from her mother, she liked that she felt vaguely Vietnamese for the first time in her life. She was even starting to like the weird smell of the house. What she didn't like was the food. She had consumed her stash of American snacks in two days, and now there were only the same, dull meals to look forward to: dragonfruit for breakfast, then rice or something soupy for lunch, and then more for din-ner later, sometimes accompanied by a piece of fish or chicken.

Thuy and Kieu never saw Grandma Tran cook—she always prepared the food while they showered and dressed, and when they came downstairs they found it already spread out on the table. Thuy felt guilty because of the element of servitude that subtly infused their relationship with their grandmother—she never ate when the girls did, only stood and watched them from the kitchen counter, and she never let them help with any of the washing up, shooing them away from the garden when they tried to fetch water for her from the pump.

Thuy's guilt was made worse by the fact that she couldn't stand the taste of her grandmother's food. She loathed the food of her people. She spent mealtimes pushing around the contents of her plate and trying not to grimace, all the while dreaming of the food back in America. To be specific, she dreamed constantly of sandwiches. She didn't know why it was sandwiches that she craved so strongly, but the thought of them began to haunt her, to obsess her. Every time she lifted her chopsticks to her lips, with every spoonful of rice gruel that she managed to choke down, she was constructing imaginary sandwiches in her head: slabs of cheese and pastrami and pink roast beef piled onto thick bread and slathered with mustard and mayonnaise.

By the middle of week two, the thoughts had utterly consumed her. Thuy knew that she was losing weight from eating—or rather not eating—Grandma Tran's cooking. When she looked in the mirror she saw how her cheeks had lost a bit of their roundness, and if she absently brought her hand to her chest she would be startled by the distinct protrusion of her collarbone. But somehow, she felt heavier than ever. And the cravings would not go away.

One afternoon, in the middle of their daily nap, Thuy suddenly awoke. Her eyes flew open and she sat straight up in the cot, jostling Kieu—who was asleep with one hand clutching Thuy's elbow—but not rousing her. Thuy's nose was tingling—she smelled something new. She thought she was imagining it at first; it was so faint against the smell of dust and motorbike exhaust from the street. But then she caught another whiff and there was no mistaking it: bread. Hot, fresh bread, with the hint of something savory underneath. She closed her eyes, lifted her nose in the air, and for a full three minutes, she sniffed. When she opened them again, she knew that she needed to find the source of it, *needed* to with an urgency that she had never experienced in her fifteen years. Thuy looked down at her arm, where Kieu was latched on firmly. She could now understand how animals snared in hunters' traps could chew off their own limbs to escape. Holding her breath the entire time, Thuy used her free hand to slowly pry Kieu's fingers off one by one. Kieu's eyelids fluttered slightly during the process, but she did not wake up. When Thuy had extricated herself successfully, she placed her sister's hand around one of the metal legs of the cot she was lying on. Like some sort of strangling jungle vine, the fingers immediately tightened around it, and Kieu, oblivious to the exchange, slept on.

Thuy stole away from the balcony with a speed she did not know she possessed. She was so eager to get away that she didn't bother looking down into the garden to see where her grandmother was. Her feet barely lighted on the stairs as she descended them. On her way down she retrieved a handful of bills from her sister's money stash in the bedroom and grabbed her sandals from the hall closet before gliding out the door and shutting it noiselessly behind her.

This was the only time of day when the street was completely deserted, save for the stray dogs that lay panting in what little shade they could find. The scent was much clearer now, and Thuy, whose stomach was pleading hungrily with her, was in its thrall. It enveloped her, intoxicated her, drew her away from her grandmother's house and into the concrete labyrinth of twisting lanes and side streets. Her footsteps quickened as the smell grew stronger, to the extent that she was practically cantering by the time she turned a corner and discovered its source.

A mud-splattered stall on wheels, with the words *Bánh mì* emblazoned on its side in red paint, stood at the end of the empty alley beneath a large green umbrella. Bánh mì, the Vietnamese sandwich, was one of the more positive souvenirs from the colonial era—a culinary hybrid of French bread, pickled Asian vegetables, pâté, and assorted meats—and though Thuy had never tasted one before, she knew it would be delicious from the smell alone.

The hot wind that had brought the scent to Thuy in the first place now spun clouds of dust around her ankles as she approached the stand. Because of the dust and the shadow cast by the umbrella, she didn't notice the figure seated on a plastic chair beside the stall until it rose to greet her. At first

Thuy wasn't sure if it was male or female: Half of the face was obscured by a conical straw hat, and a yellow kerchief was tied around the other half. Only the hands were visible—thin and brown with white scars around the knuckles, poking out from the sleeves of a drab olive work shirt buttoned to the neck. But the voice that came out from under the kerchief was sweet and gently cascading and distinctly feminine.

"Hello there," it called out in softly accented English. "You look hungry." It took Thuy a moment to realize that the words were in a language she could understand, and this both relieved and alarmed her. She froze. "Don't be shy," said the bánh mì vendor. "Here, come closer. Try some." Thuy heard the crackle of breaking bread, and then one brown hand emerged from the shadows, a hunk of baguette resting in its palm. Thuy stepped forward and took the offering, her chubby fingers trembling slightly. She suppressed the urge to hold the bread close to her nose and breathe in its warm aroma as she took the first bite but couldn't help closing her eyes as she chewed with pleasure. After two weeks of flavorless, textureless, rice-based meals, it was the most exquisite thing Thuy had ever tasted.

The vendor let out a rippling laugh, which bounced lightly off the concrete walls around them and filled the space with sound. Thuy wondered how old she actually was, beneath all those layers. "Did you like that? Let me make you a real one now. Have you ever had one before? No?"

Thuy shook her head. "We don't ever eat Vietnamese food at home," she said.

"Well, just you wait," said the woman. "One bite and you will never want to eat anything else, ever again." Her hands moved as she spoke, arranging ingredients in the shadows and chopping slivers of meat deftly with a large knife that glinted from time to time in stray sunlight. "What's your name, *con*?"

"Thuy."

"Your *full* given name."

"Well I guess it's '*Bích Thủy*,'" said Thuy, wrapping her voice with difficulty around the vowel tones. "But I go just by Thuy in the U.S. Because, um, a lot of people accidentally say 'Bich' like it's, um . . ." She lowered her voice, "'*bitch*.'" Thuy seemed relieved when the swear word didn't get a reaction from the vendor. "'Thuy' is easier," she finished weakly.

"It may be easier, but it's only half of your name. Only half the meaning," the vendor mused, as she daubed something pasty onto a baguette half, "and only half your identity. Hmm, how old are you?"

"Fifteen," answered Thuy.

"And which month were you born in?"

"April."

"Let me calculate . . . that makes you the year of the cat, correct? And how curious—I happen to be a cat as well."

She asked Thuy question after question, and Thuy, to her own amazement, responded. She wasn't sure why she was so comfortable talking with this stranger, but her words were spilling forth rapidly, so eagerly that they were practically tripping over themselves. She found herself recounting without shame that she was really in Vietnam all because she had been caught eating cake.

"Well, *con,* I don't believe there's any cake in the world that could be as delicious as this," said the vendor as she handed over the finished sandwich.

Thuy took a bite. Her eyes opened wide in wonderment. She took another, hastier bite, then another, and another, barely chewing as she gulped the bánh mì down. When she had eaten it all, the vendor made her another one, which she ate even more quickly. Something warm and light was spreading from her stomach throughout the rest of her body, flooding her, lifting her; she had the sensation that she was at once within her body and floating two inches above it. Thuy tried to pay with a couple of the crumpled bills she had taken from Kieu, but the woman refused. "Keep it," she said, closing Thuy's hand around the notes she was extending. "Talking with you was enough. I don't want your money"—she paused to wipe the blade of her knife with a checkered cloth, and when she spoke again, Thuy imagined she was smiling beneath the yellow kerchief—"just your story. Why don't you come back tomorrow at the same time? I'll make you a bánh mì even tastier than the one you had today, and you will tell me more."

Thuy nodded before she realized what she was doing. The woman continued to clean her knife slowly and deliberately, and Thuy left the alley and began retracing her steps.

When she reached the balcony, Kieu was still asleep, one

hand clinging to the leg of the empty cot. Thuy lay back down, then wriggled her hand into her sister's. The fingers squeezed hers, and a few minutes later, Kieu began to stir. She woke, looked down, saw that she was holding Thuy's hand, and then smiled. Thuy was too full to feel guilty.

HER DAYS WERE MEASURED in bánh mì now. The taste of them haunted her every hour of the day, a thousand times worse than any imagined sandwich she had concocted in her head. After spending the lunch hour rearranging the rice in her bowl with her chopsticks, Thuy would retire to the balcony with Kieu, feigning sleepiness while her stomach gurgled in anticipation. She would lie back with her eyes closed, listening as her sister's breathing slowed. Then, when she was certain that Kieu was asleep, she would free herself and disappear into the winding Saigon alleyways, her feet and her empty stomach leading her to where the sandwich vendor was always waiting. Kieu noted with dismay that Thuy's pants had gone back to fitting her snugly. "I just don't understand," she would murmur, pinching the roll of flesh at Thuy's waist. The daily bánh mì were making their presence known on Thuy's waistline, and Thuy knew it; she could feel herself bloating, growing round and bulbous like the dragonfruit she still swallowed halfheartedly at breakfast every morning.

If Grandma Tran suspected anything, she never let on. Thuy thought it should feel wrong, sneaking away as she did every day instead of staying with her grandmother—she suspected that the old woman's days were numbered, and that this was the last time they would see each other. But, Thuy reasoned to herself, wasn't it a good thing that she had found something in this country that she loved? Something new to her; something that felt uniquely her own? Wasn't it a good thing that she had a friend here? Even if she didn't know what she looked like?

It was true: Thuy had never seen the bánh mì vendor's face. She had spilled out her life story to this woman with every sandwich she gulped down, but she still didn't know what lay beneath the kerchief.

THEIR TIME IN VIETNAM passed quickly, stealthily, quietly. On the second to last afternoon, as she lay on the balcony waiting for her sister to fall asleep, Thuy suddenly realized that she hadn't thought about her home in America in a very long while. And that she didn't want to go back.

Once more she slipped out of Kieu's grasp and down the stairs to freedom. But just as her hand touched the front doorknob, she suddenly paused, sniffing warily. It was odd, she could have sworn that for a moment she had smelled a—

She turned and looked down the hallway that led to the kitchen and suppressed a shriek: Watching her through the kitchen window, dark against the violently pink flowers of the bougainvillea, was the face of her grandmother.

For several long moments, the old woman held her gaze. Then, slowly, she raised one hand—one thin, brown hand with white scars around the knuckles—and beckoned to Thuy with it. Thuy shook her head frantically, groped for the door-knob behind her, then turned and fled down the street.

"How will you be able to live without this in America?" said the sandwich vendor with a teasing edge in her voice as she handed Thuy her second bánh mì.

Thuy could not shake from her mind the image of her grandmother's face in the window. She didn't reply, just tore at the sandwich with her teeth.

The vendor watched her chew for a moment and then began cleaning her knife with her checkered cloth. "Why do you think your mother never cooks Vietnamese food?" she asked Thuy softly, without looking up.

"I don't know, and I don't care," said Thuy with her mouth full. A fat black fly buzzed near her face and she swatted at it but missed.

"Don't be like that, *con*. Think about it."

Thuy swallowed and then shrugged. "I guess . . . to protect us. No, I don't know . . . I don't know why I said that. I don't understand my mother." She stuffed the rest of the sandwich into her mouth.

"Haven't you noticed that you never talk about her?"

The fly was back and three more had joined it. Thuy waved them away with her hand before saying through her crumbs, "I don't really think about her here; she's just so far away."

To her surprise, the vendor burst out laughing, and it was

not the light ripple that Thuy had become accustomed to but a high, brittle chuckle that lasted a little too long. Thuy plucked a couple of bread crumbs from her collar and popped them into her mouth, and tried to ignore the growing sense of unease that had started somewhere at the base of her stomach and was prickling through the rest of her body. It didn't work. And when the vendor finally stopped laughing and spoke, her words caused a chill to run through Thuy despite the heat. "She *is* far away, isn't she? In another world, you could say. And there are many, many worlds within this one. Worlds alongside each other, worlds that overlap each other; you might not even know if you wandered into one that wasn't your own." With horror, Thuy noticed that more and more flies were gathering. Several had landed on the vendor's yellow kerchief, where they buzzed and crawled in dizzy patterns across the fabric, but the woman would not stop speaking. "You never talk about your mother, and your mother never talks about her life in Vietnam. She never has. But which world does she really live in, Thuy? Vietnam or America? And you, Thuy, which world do you belong to now?"

The woman covered in flies walked out from behind her stall, and Thuy recoiled when she saw that she was still holding her long knife. The woman chuckled and the flies buzzed along with her.

"Did you think I was going to hurt you?"

Thuy began to back away slowly.

"Don't you know who I am? Haven't you ever wondered why I can speak to you? Haven't you wondered why there are never any other customers here? Haven't you wondered what you've been smelling this entire time?" Then she laughed and laughed and kept laughing as Thuy sprinted away without looking back once.

After a couple of minutes Thuy slowed to a jog because she was out of breath. Then she stopped completely and looked at her surroundings. With a terrible, sinking feeling, she realized that for the first time in her life she had no idea where she was. She was as lost in this city as she would have been if she had been dropped blindfolded into the middle of a jungle. The sun had passed its zenith, and people were beginning to filter back into the streets, back to their markets and gambling corners and motorbikes. Without her grandmother there, Thuy could feel their eyes on her, mocking her, the lost girl, the fat girl, the girl who didn't belong.

She walked down alleys that seemed to coil and rearrange themselves like a knot of serpents. Her feet did not lead her home as they had done before; her nose had nothing to follow now. The streets became wider and Thuy laughed bitterly when she saw that she had ended up in front of the church from her mother's photograph. A skinny young couple in a Western wedding dress and tuxedo were posing on the steps for their own pictures. Thuy caught the bride staring at her as she passed. The streets turned narrow again and Thuy accidentally wandered into a strange house, mistaking its long, winding entryway for another alley and startling the family that lived there. Their small child started crying when he saw Thuy, and she made a hasty exit. After what felt like hours,

Thuy looked up to find that she was in front of a familiar doorstep; the city, having tired of toying with her, had deposited her at her grandmother's house once more.

As Thuy dragged herself over the threshold, she met Kieu coming down the stairs. "Oh, there you are! I woke up and you were gone. But I thought you might be with Grandma," Kieu said, wiping the sleep from her eyes.

Thuy sidestepped her and started down the hallway toward the kitchen.

"Hey! Thuy! Where are you going? What are you doing out there?"

In the garden, past the water pump, behind the lime trees and golden hibiscus and creeping tendrils of a particular flower-specked vine that had no name in English, was the body that had once been her grandmother's. Greedy black flies and a mass of wriggling white worms were fighting one another for the last of the decomposing flesh. But Thuy knew that she had been dead for about three weeks from the smell alone.

LITTLE BROTHER

—

HOW MANY TIMES HAVE I made the trip? More than the number of hairs on my head, and you see how thick it still is, even if it's white now. Back when I started the job, over forty years ago, I would leave Ca Mau at noon, when the roads were hot and empty, and wouldn't reach Saigon until dawn the next day. The roads are better now, so I could make it in seven hours if I drove without stopping. Can't, though—too old. Every two hours I need to break and take a dribbly piss in a rice paddy. Children bicycling past me while I'm stopped like to peek at the harmless, wrinkled remains of my *cặc* and giggle. "Too many women," I'll call to them. "It's all worn-out now." I usually grow sleepy somewhere between Soc Trang and Tra Vinh, so I'll sling my hammock between the truck's back tires and nap for a while.

These days I only ever get hired for boring jobs. I mostly move motorbikes and the kind of traditional carved furniture that no one actually likes to sit on. Occasionally I make the odd coconut delivery and that's about as exciting as it gets. But when the truck and I were both younger we carried anything and everything you could think of. Guns? Of course! Sometimes they heaped the open back of the pickup with AK-47s—just tossed them in like sacks of rice and didn't bother covering them up—and I would spend the entire ride listening as the guns rattled around, praying one wouldn't accidentally go off. Other times it was soldiers crammed in the cargo hold; when the sun got too hot they all took their shirts off but kept their helmets on, and when I hit potholes they would reach up to keep them on their heads in unison. In the nineties it was a lot of livestock: wooden crates of pigs and goats, and every week a huge shipment of ducks, their feet tied together, twelve stuffed in each sack, twenty-five sacks in each load. If it rained during the drive, the quacking was deafening.

Let me tell you my favorite story. Once, the son of a certain general—you'd know the name if I said it—paid me to transport a baby shark from Saigon to his house in Vinh Long. Well, they called it a baby when I took the job. I thought it might be catfish-sized, cute even. But when I came to pick it up at the docks I discovered that the beast was the size of a boat, with more teeth in its mouth than you'd want to see in a lifetime. It took me and seven other men to load the tank into the pickup. That was one of my fastest trips. I drove without sleeping and kept a bucket of fish heads in the passenger seat to feed to the thing whenever it started thrashing, for when it got restless the entire truck would shake. It was a spectacle.

Curious motorbikes followed the truck for leagues, so distracted by the creature in the tank that they almost hit each other. When I made it to Vinh Long, the general's son himself oversaw the transfer of the shark to a pool out behind the compound that could have fit most of Ca Mau inside it. While he was counting out my payment I couldn't resist asking him why he wanted such a wicked-looking fish in the first place. The general's son looked surprised that I had spoken.

After a moment he said, "I choose to keep company with monsters simply because I can." He then smiled politely, but in a way that told me it was time to go.

The hours on the road were long, but they were never really lonely. Most of the time I had somebody tagging along for a ride to the city or back from it. The ones I brought up to Saigon were always kids fresh off the farm: tired of living with their parents and looking for excitement. They seemed all the more innocent because they thought they were so worldly. The ones I returned south with were older, sadder. They had discovered that excitement is really just smog and noise and never seeing the stars, and trash piled up in the streets. They would ride with their heads out the window, their faces softening as the city fell away and the world turned flat and emerald-colored again; they were waiting for the moment when we crossed into their province, when they would smack the dashboard and cry out, "Here! Here!"

I dropped them off on the side of the highway and drove away, but I always watched in the rearview mirror as they started walking through the fields in the direction of their village. Someone else would give them a lift sooner or later.

Driving at night you have your jumpy moments, sure. From Saigon to Can Tho City there's not much except your skinny strip of asphalt cutting through rice paddy for 125 miles, and those 125 miles are very, very dark. And when things slither across the road, or weird lights bob out in the fields . . . Our grandmothers told us the stories. Our muddy patch of the world was already shadowy and blood-soaked and spirit-friendly long before the Americans got here. There's ancient and ugly things waiting to harm you in that darkness. Yes, of course they're there in daylight, too—they're just harder to spot. I'm not by any means a small man. I'm not the man you'd pick a fight with if you could help it. But I do get jittery sometimes.

Still, I've only been *really* scared once. That story's not as good as the one about the shark, but I'll tell it to you anyway, just because you're still listening.

IT WAS AFTER THE WAR, so I wasn't young anymore, but I was still good-looking enough that girls I didn't know would address me as "Older Brother," and not "Uncle." That afternoon I was up in Saigon, out by the hospital in District 5 to pick up crates of bandages, syringes, burn ointment, and cough medicine. Every month or so I would run a standard medical shipment like this.

I'd finished loading the truck and securing the crates and had turned my attention to scraping the last bits of supper from my tin—steamed pork intestines and cabbage that my wife, saintly woman, had packed for me the day before. Then from behind me, someone cleared her throat. I turned: There, standing in the doorway to the hospital, was the prettiest little thing in a starched white uniform. The nurse was peach-colored and plump in all the right places, one stockinged leg crossed behind the other, with bits of dark hair escaping from their pins and eyelashes so long they cast curving shadows on her cheeks.

"Pardon me, but are you driving south?" the girl asked, in a voice as sweet as she looked.

I put down my dinner and swallowed hard. "All the way down to Ca Mau, Little Sister. You can't go much farther south than that."

"Will you be going through Dong Thap province?"

"Dong Thap? The place is a real swamp, but I could swing through no problem, no problem at all."

"And," she left the doorway and sauntered right up to me, heels clip-clopping, "do you have room for a passenger?"

I brushed a lock of loose hair back behind her ear and her face grew hot but she didn't flinch. "I've got plenty of that," I said. This ride was going to be fun.

"I'm afraid I don't have anything to pay you with . . ."

"Oh, I don't want your money, Little Sister."

Her pink lips suddenly sharpened into a smile. "Wonderful!" she said. "I'll go get him then."

"Him?"

"Wait here." She darted back inside the hospital. Cunning little bitch. I packed up dinner and went to piss behind a bus stop, cursing quietly. When I came back she had returned with a boy who could have been anywhere from eleven to eighteen years old, possibly even older. He was dressed in a pair of faded blue pajamas; the top had no buttons so it hung open to reveal his wasted torso—the kind of skinny that I hadn't seen since the early seventies. His rib cage looked like it might break through the skin at any moment. His face was ashen, with bruise-colored rings around the eyes, and his hands shook where they dangled at his sides. But it was the way he smelled that troubled me the most. The boy was sick bad, anyone could see that, and sick people smell like sweat and shit and piss and puke. But his smell was different. Sort of cold, cold and metallic. Like a very clean knife.

"This your brother or boyfriend or something?" I asked, trying to conceal my unease.

"No, this is Minh," the nurse said cheerfully. "Minh is about to die." As if in response, Minh let his mouth fall slack and released a cough that rattled his entire body. I didn't doubt her words. "But," the nurse continued, "he wants to die back in his village. Not here, not alone in Saigon." There were tiny lines at the corners of the nurse's eyes. She wasn't nearly as young or as pretty as I'd thought. "You'll take him there." It did not appear to be a question.

I looked the kid over some more. He didn't look like he would even last the five hours to Dong Thap. I should have said no. I was going to. But when I looked down at his feet, I saw that the boy was wearing a pair of slippers fashioned out of carefully folded newspapers. It was those newspaper shoes that did me in. I couldn't refuse a poor little bastard who was inches from the grave but was still too dignified to walk around barefoot. "I'm not going to get in any trouble, right? The doctors won't mind me driving off with him like this?"

The nurse cocked an eyebrow at me. "Do you have any idea how many patients are in this hospital? We've got two to each bed, and two on mats on the floor beneath them. Honestly, the doctor'll be glad to have him gone."

"Okay. I'll do it." I climbed into the driver's seat. "But I'm doing you a big favor. This is a delivery truck, not a taxi."

The nurse led the boy around to the passenger side and helped him in. He immediately pulled his legs up to his chest in the seat and buried his face between his knees. The vertebrae of his neck jutted up like the ridges of a giant lizard. Nurse gave him a farewell pat on the head and then turned on her little white heels to leave without thanking me. After a moment she stopped mid-stride.

"Ah, Older Brother, I forgot to tell you something very important," she said, looking at me over her shoulder, one hand positioned on one round hip. I stuck my head out the window expectantly. "You shouldn't tell Minh your name. In fact, it would be better if you don't say anything to him at all. But especially not your name. If it should come up, do try to hold your tongue."

Now this was too much. "First you trick me into taking a corpse off your hands, and now you won't even let me talk to it! Giving me orders! You're more trouble than you're worth, Little Sister." I put the truck into reverse and began to pull away, and then slammed on the brake again, feeling indignant. Minh pitched forward a bit in the passenger seat but didn't fall over. "You," I called out the window, "are a bad girl. A wicked girl. And there's nothing in the world worse than that. If my wife behaved like you I would thrash her with a jackfruit skin! If I ever have a daughter I plan on beating the disobedience out of her daily! I really should teach you a lesson right here, but I'm too soft to do it."

The nurse did not appear admonished like she should have been. In fact, her face broke out into a rather toothy and unladylike grin. "Older Brother, you're *fun*," she said. "But you're wrong—there *are* some things worse than wicked girls." Her smile stretched a centimeter wider. "And they're more dangerous than you can imagine. So you'd better be careful should you encounter one of them." As I released the brake, she called out one last time, "Remember!" and then she was out of sight.

The boy remained motionless for the first hour of driving, hugging his knees with only his mop of hair visible. He coughed periodically, so I knew he wasn't dead yet. Traffic ebbed away quickly after we left the city; once we crossed the second river it was just us, the occasional motorbike, and out in the paddy the distant figures of either scarecrows or skinny farmers—you really can't tell the difference, since they both wear tattered clothes and conical hats.

After another forty-five minutes I couldn't stand it anymore. I need some noise when I'm in the truck—it doesn't have a radio, and when you spend hours driving in silence through fields that are indistinguishable from one another you start going out of your mind. You begin to wonder if you're even moving, out in the middle of all that soundless green. Times when I'm passengerless I'll just tell stories to the truck and imagine that the rumbling of the engine is it talking back because I need it, else I won't know I'm still alive. Of course I remembered what the nurse had said, about speaking to him, but there are only two kinds of people, those who can ignore their mosquito bites and those who scratch, and it's the quiet that makes me itchy.

"Little Brother . . . ," I started, unsure whether or not I had chosen the proper term of address, for I really couldn't tell his age at all. Minh slowly adjusted himself so that he was facing me but kept his head resting on his knees. I continued, "Are you hungry? I've got some leftover meat and greens in the tin down there. It's a little cold now, but you can have it if you want . . ."

I didn't think it was possible, but at the suggestion of food Minh looked even more ill. Immediately his face went lichen-colored and he looked at the container as if it were about to explode. "Okay! It's okay! I was just offering!" It was clear that a topic change was in order, and since there was really no need for tact—the boy was dying, after all—I asked him: "So what's the matter with you then?"

For the first time Minh smiled. Even his smile looked painful. "Is it not obvious? I am dying."

His voice caught me off guard: He spoke clearly and strangely formally, with a clipped northern accent that you rarely heard around these parts of the delta. "Erm. Yes. But *why* are you dying? Did the doctors tell you what it was?" I kicked myself for having forgotten to ask the nurse if it was catching or not.

"My current body is simply too sick to continue living. So now I am dying."

"Yes, but . . . Oh never mind." Something was apparently wrong with the boy's head as well. He probably had some new disease, from America or Europe. But I've never had a sickness I couldn't cure with the proper amount of rice wine, so I wasn't that worried. The minutes passed slowly and silence returned, gloating.

Desperate, I tried again. "What was the hospital like?"

To my surprise he raised his entire head when he replied. "Filthy. Vile. Foul. There were no healthy people to talk to and I was always hungry." The very memory of the place caused Minh to relapse; he dropped his head back between his knees and released five coughs—short, hoarse barks—in quick succession.

I figured that that would be the end of our conversation, and that Minh would go back to silence, preserving his last dregs of energy. So I was taken aback when, after a few moments, his face reappeared. We were heading southwest, and in the orangey light of the setting sun he even looked slightly healthier. "Older Brother," he asked me, "have you been a deliveryman long?"

"Almost twenty years," I said. Even though he'd caught me off guard I attempted a clumsy lure: "So I must have been at the job before you were even born, right?"

Minh didn't fall for it and instead went on as if he hadn't heard the question. "Will you tell me about it?"

I slowed the truck down a little. "The years on the road? There isn't much to tell, and what there is isn't interesting . . . ," I began, and cleared my throat.

Minh looked at me blankly. "Why would you say that, when you are smiling and it is plain that you have been waiting this whole time to talk about yourself?"

I almost swerved off the road, hearing those words coming from someone who was my junior. But there was no impudence in his voice. He sounded genuinely puzzled. When he saw the shock on my face he said, "I now understand; it was self-deprecation meant to ease me into your story. Continue."

How do you respond to something like that? I certainly didn't know. After a long, awkward minute, Minh saved me the trouble of stammering out some sort of response. "I gather from your silence that I have caused you to be embarrassed and I apologize. Please say something. Hearing your voice lends me strength."

I shrugged. "Well, I'm flattered, I guess. What would you like me to tell you about?"

"I want you to give me your life story, beginning with your birth and ending here, in this truck. Tell it however you will, but omit as little as possible. I will not interrupt you."

"I suppose I can do that." I took a deep breath and began. "I was born in Ca Mau." I looked at him out of the corner of my eye. His face was cast with weirdly shaped shadows from the sunset behind him, and his profile had gone hazy at the edges in its light. He was staring dead ahead with his mouth dangling open, which I found mildly unsettling. I turned my attention back to the road and kept talking, more as a way to forget about my odd passenger than to fulfill his request.

"It feels strange to be the one speaking. Usually the people riding with me only want to talk about themselves and their big plans for when they get to the city or get away from it. When they speak to me it's like me speaking to my truck. I wouldn't think that a person getting ready to die would want to hear someone else's life story. A dying man tells his own stories to anyone and everyone on the off chance that later on, one of them will remember he existed. A dying man shouldn't have time to listen to a man like me. But you're not like the others, are you?" I looked over at him again but he had not moved. "I honestly can't tell if you're bored or if you're gobbling up every word out of my mouth. Maybe you're just too sick to talk anymore." Still no reaction. He was being true to his word about not interrupting me. "I was the fourth of seven children. It's fitting that I'm the middle child—the three older siblings went off one by one to work in Saigon, the youngest three stayed in Ca Mau and took care of our parents, and I've spent my life driving back and forth between the two."

When we drove through Tan An, I was six years old and having my legs caned for stealing mangoes from a neighbor's tree.

Waiting for the My Tho ferry I was fourteen and as a joke dumped a pot of water on a female classmate. The thin fabric of her white school uniform turned translucent and exposed her tiny breasts.

Crossing into Ben Tre I was nineteen and marrying her.

Leaving it I was almost twenty-five and driving down the highway with a shark in the back of my truck.

I was talking so much that I didn't realize how late it had gotten. And how dark. Three motorbikes passed us in streaks of yellow light and briefly lit up the coconut trees lining the highway. I could smell a river in the near distance.

"Minh—" I stopped and coughed. My voice was hoarse, probably from speaking for too long. I tried again. "Minh, let's stop for a minute. I . . . I feel . . . tired. All of a sudden."

I pulled the truck over and stepped onto the road. And then, without warning, both my legs gave out. I held myself up on the door until, to my surprise, Minh himself came over and took my weight on one of his shoulders. I worried that I was hurting him but had no choice but to lean against him. He walked me over toward the trees and lowered me onto the ground because I could no longer stand.

"I don't know what's wrong," I said, rubbing my legs. "Out of nowhere I went all—" I was interrupted by a dry coughing fit that lasted over a minute. "I went all weak. Why am I so dizzy?"

His voice from the shadows: "You were sitting for several hours. It is normal."

Perhaps it was because he had been silent for so long, but his voice sounded lower to me. In any case I couldn't respond because I was coughing again.

Minh stood on the shoulder of the road instead of on the grass. It was probably for the best—the ground had muddy patches and his shoes were made of newspaper. "Driving is difficult work, Older Brother. Your life has been a hard one. It's time to rest now."

"Strange way to put it, but—*cough*—you're—*cough cough*—right."

"Older Brother, I know everything else about you, but you still have not told me your name."

I remembered the words of the nurse again and hesitated. Lucky I did, for just then a motorbike drove by and its headlight illuminated the two of us. And in that sudden instant of light I saw that something about Minh had changed. When we left Saigon, the boy's cheeks had been sunken, his eyes hollow, his skin gray and drooping. But somehow, miraculously, the face was now full and fresh. His eyes had become bright and alert; the dark rings beneath them had vanished. He looked like an entirely different person. I jerked away from him.

"Is something wrong, Older Brother?"

Everything was wrong. His face, my body, whatever was happening to us. I tried to stand but my legs were still not my own and my head swam. I started crawling away from Minh on my hands and knees instead, and for the first time he laughed.

He let me make it a couple of yards before he walked carefully over, feeling for dry spots before putting a foot down. He kicked me onto my back with one newspaper-clad foot. Even in the dark I could tell that he had grown larger, his chest and shoulders broader.

"Now, will you tell me your name or do I need to search the truck for your license and find it that way?"

The soft spluttering of an engine in the darkness: Another motorbike was approaching. This time I was ready. I was staring up at the shadow where I knew Minh's face was when the light came. When I saw it, I did not scream. I would tell you if I had—I am not ashamed—but I could not make a sound.

It was my face. He had my face. The features of it—my lips, my nose, the ridge of my forehead—were lumpier, fleshier, but I knew with sickening certainty that the face I was looking up at was a replica of my own.

"Do you like it?" He smiled and I caught a glimpse of a crooked left canine as the last of the light faded. I ran my tongue over the bumpy spot in the corner of my own mouth.

But that wasn't even the most frightening part. What scared me the most—what still haunts me to this day—was what happened next.

"What is my name?" he asked quietly.

At these words it wasn't "Minh" but *my own name* that rose involuntarily to my lips, because in that moment it was no longer mine. And this response was mechanical, something that I—or whoever I was in that instant, for I had ceased to be myself—did not question. My mind was no longer my own. Nothing will ever be as profoundly terrifying as that moment. That feeling of . . . not of possession, but of dispossession. I can explain it to you in no other way.

I didn't say it—do you think I would be here now if I had? Just as the words were preparing to leave my throat, they were interrupted: My body, in one desperate, final act of defense, suddenly lurched and divested itself of my dinner. Partially digested pork intestine and bits of cabbage and rice disgorged themselves with impressive momentum and splattered all over Minh, who was looming above me. Again, I am not ashamed. I was lucky; you don't get to be my age in this country without luck and a high tolerance for what makes others squeamish. The physical effort required for such powerful vomiting left me spent, so I could only sprawl weakly on the grass and watch, baffled, as Minh completely lost it.

First he staggered backward, gasping for air. I understood that—the smell was overwhelmingly foul. But then he threw his head back and shrieked—a horrible, animal sound that cut through the night. He flailed and twisted and slapped at his body wildly. It looked like he was fighting off a swarm of bees, not trying to flick away bits of sick.

"No no no no no," he said over and over again, until his words didn't sound like words anymore. When he threw himself down and began rolling frantically, wiping his body on the ground, I found the strength to begin dragging myself across the grass on my stomach like a serpent. Every movement was exhausting and my body was still shaking with fear, but Minh didn't notice that I was escaping. I could see him thrashing in the darkness at the edge of my vision. As I inched along the ground my fingers touched something damp and papery—one of Minh's little shoes that he had kicked off during his flailing fit. I clutched it in my hand and managed to pull myself up to my feet. Without really knowing why, I put the shoe into my pocket. Then I walked unsteadily back to the truck and climbed in, trying and failing twice to close the door before finally getting it shut. The key was still in the ignition.

I didn't want to look at him when I started the engine and the headlights came on. Couldn't help it, though. He had torn off his blue pajama top and was scrubbing furiously at his chest with it. His hair swung in front of his face with each angry motion, or stuck to it in sweaty hanks, hiding it. I know it was probably just the poor light, but to me he looked blurry around the edges. Like the image on a cheap television. As I drove off I watched his figure in the rearview mirror grow smaller and smaller until it finally disappeared, leaving only a corner of my own face and a fading triangle of road in the glass. I wondered if somebody would stop and offer him a ride. Then, tentatively, I stretched out my neck to examine the rest of my reflection. It was not, as I had feared, Minh's face that looked back at me from the mirror, but I was covered in a putrid mask of the now-crusting throw-up.

I crossed into the next province. There aren't any signs at the borders, but when you've been driving as long as I have you just know these things. A skinny branch of river ran alongside the road; the truck lights glanced off the surface of the water at points where the bank was sparse and so close that if you oversteered by an inch you'd be swimming. I pulled over and parked. Flexed the muscles in my thighs a couple of times. Thought that I felt like myself again, but wasn't sure that I was entirely the self I was before. I stepped out of the truck and tested my legs again. Walked toward the water.

Even in the darkness the river didn't look a healthy color. I stood at the bank and stripped off my filthy clothes, trying not to think about what could be in that water. Snakes, broken glass, the shit of half a dozen villages upstream. My feet were swallowed by mud the moment I entered, and each step made a sucking sound. What I hoped were tiny fish darted around my ankles. When I was in up to the thighs, I squatted down and began to wash, cupping the water in my hands and splashing it onto my body, and when that was too slow, I completely submerged myself. I scrubbed my face, feeling the scabs of dried vomit loosen and come off my skin, and ran my fingers through the gunk in my hair until it was gone. Even though the water smelled funny and left a gritty brownish residue on every inch of me, I'd never felt cleaner in my life. It was getting chilly, though, and I wanted to get out before some aquatic creature started nibbling on my cặc, so I squelched my way back to shore. I shook myself dry like a dog, spraying droplets everywhere. My clothes were too foul to put back on so I kicked them into the river, but first I took the newspaper shoe out of my pocket and cradled it in my hands. Then I set it gently down in the water and blew it away from the shore. It looked like a tiny boat bobbing into the darkness.

I got back in the truck, naked as the day I was born and feeling just as new. It sounds crazy, but I think that at *that* moment, if I had decided to forget the truth about Minh, the truth about what had just happened and everything I'd seen, I could've done it, simply by wanting it gone. Just driven off and abandoned the memories in that little corner of the delta, and twenty years later I wouldn't even be able to remember the name of the sick boy I'd driven once, or the reason why we never made it to Dong Thap.

I let my fingers rest on the key for a moment before turning it with a sigh that was lost in the sound of the engine coming to life. I readjusted my rearview mirror even though I could see nothing in the heavy black night behind me.

NOW THAT YOU'VE heard everything, you know that I chose to keep them. The nurse with the soft curves and the pointed smile. Minh and his newspaper shoes. My own face looming above me. They're with me still. I've had them stored in my head this whole time and it's like having another shark in the back of my truck, but this time I don't know where I'm taking it. I just keep driving and hope it won't get restless, because I'm too scared to feed it.

THE RED VEIL

———

I DON'T WANT TO BORE YOU with my own history, with the reasons that I joined the order and the chronicles of my meandering faith; that is not my purpose here. But some background is, I feel, necessary. I sought out Sister Emmanuel during the first year of my novitiate because I was considering leaving the convent. I didn't want to approach Mother Superior for guidance: She was the classic Catholic nightmare, barking after naughty schoolboys with her ruler in hand. Sister Emmanuel was quiet, and from time to time I encountered her taking early morning walks around the garden of the Stations of the Cross. She was a stoop-backed woman with white hair and nut-brown skin crosshatched with wrinkles, and she was always wearing a kind smile and an enormous pair of dark, square sunglasses. I had never seen her without the glasses—she even wore them during Mass—and for this she had acquired secret nicknames like "Sister Kim Jong-il" and "the Terminator" from some of the younger nuns. But to me she seemed—then, at least—to be at peace. Contemplative. Diligent. Devout. In short, she was all that I wished to be, and was failing at being.

I found her on a Saturday in the kitchen, preparing egg rolls to bring to the parish soup kitchen. She had her sleeves rolled up to her elbows and her hands deep in a bowl of minced meat and mushrooms and noodles. It was a bright, cold day, and the sun from the window over the sink silhouetted her dark, hunched form. She looked up when I entered the room, but I couldn't tell if she was surprised to see me or not; her sunglasses, as usual, were perched on her nose. I tried to explain myself rationally and calmly, but there was an involuntary tremble of emotion in my voice. Sister Emmanuel said nothing during my monologue, and continued to mix the egg roll filling while listening to my presentation. But when I trailed silent, having revealed the turbulence in my mind, she removed her hands from the bowl, wiped them on a checked dishcloth, and then folded them in front of her. For the first time she smiled.

"Would it shock you very much," she said, "if I told you that I don't believe in God?"

I hadn't known exactly what to expect, but I knew that it wasn't this. She continued: "I want to help you, but I have no answers. All I have is a story. I've never told it to anyone before and I think it's time. You may take what you like from it; look for a moral if you can. Perhaps the story will give you something, though you must be careful lest you give yourself to it instead."

And as she told it to me she began to roll the filling in paper-thin wrappers, her voice rising and falling with the movements of her hands.

I WILL START at the very beginning—the beginning we all were taught as children.

Thousands of years ago, a dragon prince and a fairy spirit fell in love. They married, and the fairy bore one hundred eggs, which hatched into one hundred beautiful children. However, the dragon lived beneath the sea, while the fairy's home was in the mountains, and they could not be together. Fifty of the children went to live with their mother in the high hills of the North, and fifty of the children went south to the coast, where they learned to fish and make boats while their father watched over them from his palace beneath the waves. These children were the first people of Vietnam.

There is a place very close to the center of my country where the green fingers of the southern mountains almost touch the sea. The water there used to be the loveliest in all of the country—warm, clear, and teeming with fish. The buildings of the fishing hamlet by the bay were painted pink and green and turquoise, and the crumbling remains of a Cham temple overlooked it all from the hills. On the outskirts, where the town began to give way to jungle, in a yellow, colonial house, Vu Nguyen's wife was giving birth. Huong came from a long line of beautiful and tempestuous women, and she thrashed and let out long, guttural screams while Mrs. Dang, the midwife, tried to calm her. Vu was pacing out by a bamboo grove in the yard, trying to ignore the sounds from inside and occasionally looking up at the rainclouds curdling in the sky. It was the beginning of the monsoon season.

Eventually, there was silence from the house. Vu drew in a long breath, looked up at the dark sky, exhaled, then turned and went in. He came across Mrs. Dang first; she was in the kitchen making a pot of tea, and Vu blanched when he saw that she had not washed her hands. He was a very slight man, and at the sight of her fingers and forearms stained with red he almost fell over.

"Anh Vu, congratulations! I'll bring you a chicken for supper." In addition to being the local midwife, Mrs. Dang bred noisy brown chickens that were always escaping from their pen and running loose in the streets. "Now go in and see your children!" She grinned at him with betel-nut–stained teeth.

"My *children*?"

"Ai-ya!" Mrs. Dang exclaimed, striking her forehead with her hand and accidentally smearing it with red. "How stupid— I spoiled the surprise!"

Vu rushed into the bedroom, where he found Huong and his surprise. His wife's hair was matted and sweaty, and she had a cigarette in her mouth and two little bundles in her arms. Twins. Timidly, he approached their little trinity.

"They're girls, Vu," said Huong, exhaling a gray ribbon of smoke. "I know that's not what you wanted. And there's two of them."

Vu came over and sat on the edge of the bed, carefully

avoiding the soils from the birth on the sheets. The babies were awake and blinking their eyes—blue eyes in dark faces. Milky blue eyes, like those of Siamese cats. Outside, the distant rainstorm rumbled. Vu shuddered.

He named the girls Vi and Nhi.

UNLIKE OTHER CHILDREN'S, Nhi's and Vi's eyes never changed to brown. People whispered that it was from the French blood on their mother's side, and that there was a strain of the French madness in them, too. They were such strange children, strange and quiet. As infants they rarely cried, and when relatives and well-wishers came by to congratulate Vu and Huong, they didn't like to linger too long after they met the girls. There was something deeply unsettling about their identical, silent blue stares.

Even as they grew older they never really spoke to anyone except each other. Huong took to locking herself in the bedroom most days with a bottle of rice spirits or occasionally one of her lovers, and Vu, resigned to the fact that he had lost his wife, devoted himself to his job as a civil servant. The twins were left to themselves. They would play in the forest, around the ruins on the hill, or go down to the beach and catch and torture crabs. Sometimes they fought with each other, kicking and biting savagely, not out of anger but boredom. They would alternate which one of them would win.

They began to disappear for days at a time, returning to the yellow house hungry and dirty and with secrets. If they encountered their mother on one of her rare excursions from the bedroom, she would immediately stick them both into the bath.

"*Chim con*—my baby birds," she would mutter. "Chim, why can't you be *good*?" Then she would go off to find soap and leave them in the tub for hours, and when she remembered them they were gone again.

ONE SUNNY AFTERNOON, Vi went looking for Mrs. Dang. She found her out in the chicken pen holding a brown clay jar in one hand.

"Which one are you?" said Mrs. Dang, narrowing her beady black eyes at Vi.

"Nhi," lied Vi.

"Eh," said Mrs. Dang, and took a swig from the jar. "I knew it—you're the skinnier one. How old are you now?"

"Eight." This was true.

"Ai-ya! How time flies! What is it you want, precious?" In addition to being the local midwife and chicken breeder, Mrs. Dang peddled home remedies and medicine she got at half price from a relative in the Saigon black market.

"Huong is having the same sickness as last time." They never called her "mother."

"Again, eh? Take a bottle of my special tea from the counter in the kitchen. But first, watch how I get my dinner." With a serpentine strike of her hand, Mrs. Dang caught a chicken by the neck and shoved its beak into the jar, forcing it to drink.

After a minute it stopped struggling. "It's drunk," Mrs. Dang said, placing the chicken on the ground and then taking a quick swig for herself from the jar. The creature staggered sideways. "So it won't feel a thing." She stroked its head and then, with practiced swiftness, wrung its neck.

Vi left when Mrs. Dang began plucking it. She took a brown glass bottle of dark liquid from inside and walked back toward the dirt road. Nhi was waiting for her by the gate and wordlessly joined her. They took turns holding the bottle on the way home.

Huong was curled up on the bedroom floor, smoking, with the curtains drawn. There was a broken vase next to her, and a bloody clump of black hair was stuck to the wall. When Nhi and Vi opened the door to the room they recoiled at the sight. Their mother's face was obscured by the clouds of cigarette smoke, and her bathrobe had fallen open.

"Chim? Is that you?" She struggled to sit up and tuck her breasts inside the robe. The room stank. "Bring that here, Chim con. Your *mẹ*'s head hurts very much." There was an oozing bald patch on her scalp.

The twins inched closer, Vi holding the bottle out toward their mother. Huong stretched out her arm to take it, but then suddenly pitched forward and grabbed Nhi's ankle instead. Both girls froze. Huong's grip tightened and her nails dug into her daughter's skin, making her wince. Then Huong's head flopped down and her hold went slack. Nhi dropped the bottle on the wooden floor, where it bounced but did not break and then rolled toward the bed. Without lifting her head, Huong began to grope around for the bottle, her pale hand scuttling across the floorboards, and when her girls fled from the room she did not notice.

The next morning, Mrs. Dang decided to pay a visit to their house, a plucked chicken tucked under her arm as a present. No one answered her knocks, so she opened the door and went in. She wrinkled her nose at the odor that greeted her, and followed it to the bedroom. When she pushed open the door, her face froze and she dropped the chicken: Huong was lying dead in a puddle of vomit on the floor. Mrs. Dang shuffled over and picked up the empty bottle near her. Her eyes grew wide. After she had calmed herself down she retrieved the chicken, went outside, and tossed the bottle deep into the bamboo thicket at the far end of the backyard. Only then did she go out into the street and begin wailing for help.

IT TOOK ME ALMOST a full minute to realize that Sister Emmanuel had stopped speaking. The egg rolls lay finished in rows on the tabletop; the old nun's hands were still. Through the window I could see that the sun was now red and bobbing on the edge of the horizon.

"That seems like more than enough, doesn't it?" she finally said. She paused, and then something that could have been a smile twisted her mouth and she continued, gesturing at the egg rolls, "They'll never be able to eat all of these." She started to cover them with aluminum foil. Because I could not find anything to say, I took the mixing bowl over to the sink and began to rinse it. My fingers felt clumsy and stiff.

"When do you fry them?" I asked eventually.

"Later," said Sister Emmanuel. "They're much better served hot." There was a pause before she added, "On Thursday I will need to make another batch for the parish potluck." She left the kitchen without another word.

That night, for the first time since my initial vows, I did not say my prayers.

On Thursday Sister Emmanuel was waiting in the convent kitchen, seated at the table, which, to my surprise, was empty. "Hello, Sister," she greeted me serenely. "Do not sit down just yet."

My hand hovered awkwardly above the chair I had been reaching for.

"I would like you to assemble the ingredients for me. Do you remember them?"

I couldn't help but feel that this was some sort of test. Though I had only a dim notion of what went into the egg rolls, I feared that if I failed to complete the task, she would not continue her story. Trepidatiously, I began selecting ingredients from the refrigerator and cupboards, trying to think back to what I had seen and smelled in the kitchen during our last meeting. Sister Emmanuel's face, or the few parts of it that weren't concealed by the glasses, betrayed nothing as I placed each of the items on the table. I finished by setting down the chopping knife, the cutting board, and the mixing bowl. Then

I stood waiting for her judgment with my hands folded. Every so often my fingers twitched nervously.

Sister Emmanuel scanned the collection. "Very well done, Sister," she said. "You only missed one ingredient." Disappointment welled up in my chest. "A small thing," she continued, rising from her chair and crossing the room; "a humble ingredient, and easily overlooked." She returned from the refrigerator holding a single egg. "But this is what binds the entire creation together."

The shell glowed yellow in the afternoon light. She cracked it into the bowl and then resumed her story.

IN THOSE DAYS the law did not look kindly upon anything that could be termed the "unnatural," for it was believed to have a dangerous effect on the general public. If the police had known that the notorious Red Woman of the North would be passing through town they surely would have tried to apprehend her, for she claimed to be a powerful seer with the entire spirit world at her disposal. But she was wily and she was feared. She went by a hundred different names, and in the stories they told of her she was sometimes a wizened old crone, sometimes young and sylphlike. Sometimes she was not wholly woman, and usually she could change shape. She had never been caught.

The news of her arrival spread quietly, quickly through the village. It moved like a disease: exchanged with the vegetables at the marketplace, whispered between neighbors, passed around on scraps of paper at the local school. Red Woman was stopping for a single night during her journey down the coast. She would demonstrate her power to communicate with the dead, and even to grant them speech again, for a price. There would be only one show. The old temple after sundown; one piaster per person.

Nhi and Vi were thirteen, just becoming beautiful, and the news had made its way to them from one of the young, shaggy-haired fishermen at the docks who stared for too long and raised their voices whenever they passed. At moonrise, they made their way to the Cham temple on the hill. Vi and Nhi linked arms as they approached, Nhi sweeping a long branch in front of them on the path, for snakes. There was rustling jungle to either side of them, and a noisy silence in the darkness like the sound of a held breath. A light, faintly fishy breeze was blowing in from the sea—monsoon season was still a ways off. When they reached the crumbling archway they each handed a coin to a little man wearing old army fatigues, the pants rolled up to the knees. He grinned at them as they entered, and they were treated to a view of his many missing teeth.

For hundreds of years the nearby banyan trees had been slowly strangling the temple—their roots grew up through the bricks and around the columns like long gray fingers. Inside, in the middle of the central chamber, a fire on a grate cast ruddy light on carvings of monkey guards, grinning demons, and dancing goddesses. Nhi and Vi took a place on the floor and looked around at the other villagers who had come:

mostly men and curious children, but there were some women there, too—both young and old—and the twins knew that several of them were there to try to speak with their husbands or sons who had been soldiers. These women stood near the back, where the shadows hid their hollow faces.

In front of them all, before the fire, squatted the largest, darkest woman they had ever seen. She had shoulders as broad as a water buffalo's, and sinewy forearms that were folded in front of her chest. The firelight flickered off her russet-colored face, immobile as the stone carvings on the wall, and points of flame were reflected in two black, glassy eyes. Her eyebrows were shaved off, and she wore a red silk scarf twisted turban-like around her head. Behind her loomed the tall sandstone sculpture of a grimacing creature that looked to be half lion, half dragon.

The smiling man waited a moment longer for stragglers, counted the money, and stowed it away in a hidden pocket. He strode in, arms spread wide, and spoke.

"Mesdames, messieurs! Welcome!" He had a strange hiss in his voice, and Nhi and Vi weren't sure if it was his missing teeth or an accent they could not place. "Thisss night, can you not feel the spiritsss? They are, hmmm . . ." He paused, closed his eyes, and sniffed at the air like an animal. Then he opened his eyes again, winked, and darted sideways into the darkness of the temple recess. There were confused murmurs from the audience, and people looked around, waiting for him to reappear. Then they heard a chuckle coming from above them. He was seated astride the neck of the lion-dragon, leaning his elbows on its stone head with his hands laced under his chin. He leered down at them, flashing his black gums. Then he continued: "They are . . . everywhere—they swarm. And perhapsss your own loved one is among them, ah? With a messs-sage for you, hmmm? Or perhapsss they have something that mussst be finished . . ." He let his words die out slowly and allowed an uncomfortable silence to fill the space before whispering, "Now, the misstressss of the spiritssss; the woman who can crosssss between our world and theirs."

He vaulted from the dragon and into the shadows again as the enormous Red Woman rose. In one fluid motion, she unraveled the scarf from around her head, releasing a curtain of dark hair that fell past her waist. She shook out the red silk in front of her, and there was a curious symmetry in the black shroud of her hair and the scarlet shroud in her hands. Red Woman spoke, her voice low, hoarse, and halting.

"To bring the spirits I must cover myself. They will only speak through the faceless; they will not be seen by our eyes . . ."

She lifted the cloth high, then lowered it over her head, where it draped fluidly down over her torso, turning the woman into a smooth pillar of red that glowed in the light of the flames. For several long minutes everything was still, save for the occasional animal scream from the trees outside the temple and the fidgeting of the audience within. Suddenly Red Woman began to chant in a low drone that echoed off the stone and vibrated deep in the chests of all in the audience: strange, rippling syllables that sounded as if they had three or four pitches at once. Time was twisted with the sound, and no one was sure how many minutes passed before, with a sharp intake of breath, the chanting ended as abruptly as it had begun. Silence descended again. But then a new voice, high and quivering, from beneath the veil:

"Chim?"

At the word, Nhi's shoulders immediately hunched up. Vi clenched her teeth and her eyes narrowed.

"Chim con? Chim? Where are you?" The figure in the sheet was now moving toward them with lurching steps.

"Such naughty little girls. You never listened. Tell me you're sorry. Very bad. Very bad girls. Why won't you come here? Chim?" It was right in front of them now, red and rippling and horrible. The villagers in the audience couldn't agree on what happened next. Some said that it was one of the twins who yanked off the veil. Others said that they saw the fabric snag on the stone claws of one of the temple's statues. There even were a few who claimed later that a long, thin shadow crept out of the forest and did it. But they all saw the same thing when the cloth fell away: Red Woman's head was thrown back and her eyes were rolled up into her skull, all whites; her hands twitched and rhythmically clenched and unclenched. A trickle of foam was starting at the corner of her mouth.

In the audience some shrieked, some found their voices dried up in their throats, some leapt to their feet, others were paralyzed where they sat. None of them could tear their eyes away from the convulsing figure of Red Woman. "Help her!"

someone cried out from the back, but no one seemed willing to physically touch the woman, whose shaking was growing stronger.

It must have been during the commotion that the wind—cooler and saltier than before—began to pick up. It set the fire in the grate flickering violently but did not put it out. It lashed Nhi's and Vi's hair in front of their eyes. The red fabric rose from where it had puddled on the floor and wafted first into a far corner of the temple, where it fluttered for a moment from a spire-like carving, and then with another gust it was whipped away into the night. It was only then that Red Woman stopped shaking. Softly, for such a large woman, she dropped to her knees, then pitched face-forward into the fire. It was then that the man with the missing teeth leapt out from the shadows and yanked her back by the shoulders, but he wasn't fast enough—the acrid stench of burning skin and hair filled the temple, and the seer was bellowing in agony with both hands clasped to her face. When she let her hands fall away, a wail of horror rose from the audience and echoed off the ancient stones.

Nhi and Vi were already on their feet and making for the jungle, but they turned to look back over their shoulders at the sound. Though they were halfway through the temple arch, they could still see Red Woman's face clearly: The coals had seared away the flesh around one eye, and the socket was black and gaping like a second screaming mouth. In unison, the twins turned away again and ran into the darkness.

———

"Why, Sister, what are you doing?" Sister Emmanuel suddenly exclaimed.

"What? I'm not doing anything!" I protested.

Sister Emmanuel gave me a funny look. "Your hands, Sister," she said softly.

I looked down at the tabletop where I had been resting my forearms. With a shock, I saw that my hands were moving strangely, clenching and then relaxing in a slow but relentless rhythm, the wrists rolling backward and forward each time my fingers tightened. I had been so engrossed in the story that I had not noticed.

Sister Emmanuel wiped her own hands off on a dishcloth and then placed them on top of mine. My body shuddered, and the clenching stopped. "Perhaps that is enough for today," Sister Emmanuel said, rising from her chair. It took me an awfully long time to realize that I was alone in the kitchen.

We had not made a plan to meet again, but when I came to the kitchen the following afternoon, she was there. The egg roll filling was already prepared, but this time it had been divided between two mixing bowls. "Here," she said, sliding one over to me as I took my place at the table. "You are ready to make them, too."

I looked down at my clumsy hands. I had woken up several times in the night to find them moving of their own accord at my sides. "But I don't know how!" I protested.

"Of course you do." Sister Emmanuel readjusted her sunglasses, then sank her hands into the bowl. "I have been teaching you."

IN THE YEARS SINCE his wife's death, Vu had grown increasingly detached from the world outside his routine of work, sleep, and two bowls of rice daily. He became a colorless, insubstantial man. Each morning the townspeople would watch Old Vu ride his rickety bicycle to the office—his back bent, his head lowered, his bony knees looking like they were about to pierce through the material of his baggy, grayish suit with every pedal—and each evening they would watch him ride home again. He never spoke to anyone, not even to Mrs. Dang when she came over with a plump hen to try to entice him into eating more.

"The man's not long for this world," she would say to anyone who would listen. "One day I'll find him dead in that house, and I don't know if my weak old heart will be able to take another shock like that—I was the one who found Huong, you know? Have I told you that story before? What a tragedy, eh? And a mystery, too—no one has any idea what killed the poor woman, no idea at all . . ."

Naturally, it came as a surprise to everyone when Old Vu quietly announced that he was going to remarry. The woman was a religion teacher at a school in Cam Ranh, never married and now past her prime, who had answered the newspaper advertisement that Old Vu had placed a few months back.

There were no apparent benefits to the union—neither was particularly wealthy, and Vu's hair had been white for years while the schoolteacher was rumored to be exceptionally plain.

"At least his back is so stooped that he'll never have to see her face," the townspeople whispered among each other. "But what do you think she'll do when she meets the girls?"

Vi and Nhi were the last ones to find out about their father's new bride. In fact, they did not know that there was to be a wedding until the very day of the ceremony. An unspoken agreement existed between the twins and their father, and they had managed to cross paths only a handful of times in over two years. Old Vu left for work before Nhi and Vi woke up in the morning, and they were gone long before he came home in the evening. The twins were now sixteen and menacingly beautiful. They didn't go to school; they had no interest in housework or cooking. They maintained the same half-feral existence that they had as children, spending their time traipsing around the jungle or the beaches, except now they stayed far, far away from the temple on the hill. When they needed to sleep, they slept. When they needed to eat, there was leftover rice in the pot or a jar of money in the corner of the kitchen that Old Vu left for them. Sometimes they would make an appearance in town, walking with their heads held high and their arms linked, relishing the stares of the bystanders. The twins had a weakness for mangosteens and would buy several dozen at a time, meeting the curious gaze of the fruit seller with two pairs of narrow blue eyes that lacked anything resembling human warmth. Then they would swing themselves easily into a high tree and eat their fruits, throwing the dark purple peels at anyone who happened to come too close.

Mrs. Dang, who had long given up trying to socialize the girls, was the one who informed Nhi and Vi of the impending nuptials. On the morning of the wedding, she came by the yellow house dressed in her best ao dai to find the twins curled up asleep beneath the kitchen table. The soles of their feet were caked with black mud and their hair was tangled together.

"Ai-cha! Get up, the pair of you! Your new stepmother will be here very soon!" Mrs. Dang prodded Nhi, the nearest one, with the pointed toe of her special-occasion embroidered slippers. The girls crawled out from underneath the table and stood, stretching their necks and shaking out their long, slender limbs like egrets in a rice paddy. The news did not appear to elicit a reaction from Nhi or Vi, but as Mrs. Dang supervised their cleaning and dressing—she didn't trust them to get the job done by themselves—she noticed that their eyes kept meeting over the washbasin, as if communicating something that she was not privy to.

Despite the fact that Mrs. Dang and the twins were the only audience members in attendance, the schoolteacher from Cam Ranh had the church filled with flowers and wore a white, Western-style dress, complete with a train and lace veil. "These foolish modern women," Mrs. Dang clucked to herself from a pew. The bride had also chosen to forgo the traditional tea ceremony and bowing before the ancestral altar, which Mrs. Dang thought most unwise. She doubted that they had even consulted their astrological charts before becoming engaged.

Nhi and Vi slipped out of the church silently before the final vows. They hadn't even seen the bride's face.

IT TURNED OUT that Xuan, the new wife, was just as plain as the rumors had predicted, with heavy, sunken cheeks, a thick waist, and hair coarse as straw that she always pulled back into a severe bun. But her eyes sparkled with intelligence and she carried herself differently from the other women. With them, you could see it in the curve of their spines—the weight of generations of famine, of husbands and brothers and sons leaving home for war and never coming back. Xuan may have had the plodding features of a peasant, but she possessed a lightness that they did not. Old Vu could not love her—he was far too out of practice for that—but he could fear her a little. Not the same fear that he had felt for his old wife, with her fits of wailing and drunkenness and violence, but a kind of formless anxiety, the feeling one gets setting out for home after the sun has already begun to set, of trying to outrace the darkness. He supposed it meant that he cared for her. They took walks together, they ate the meals that Xuan cooked together, they slept together in the bed where the twins had been born, on the mattress that still had a burn hole from when Huong had once tried to set fire to it with a cigarette. Old Vu was certain that they were doing everything a good married couple should. Still, he could not shake the sense of apprehension that he felt whenever he interacted with his new wife. When he was at home he tended to lapse into silence and just watch her moving about, him trying to give a name to the strange dread he felt. But no one watched her more warily than the twins.

They lurked in the bushes, they stared at her from the shadows. Now that she lived in the house, they didn't sleep under the kitchen table anymore; because it was the dry season they moved to the roof, peering at her through gaps in the thatching that Old Vu had neglected to mend, spying silently until they fell asleep beneath the stars.

In her own way, Xuan studied the girls just as closely as they studied her. She noticed that the burnt rice crust at the bottom of the pot vanished whenever she wasn't paying attention, and she noticed the muddy footprints that appeared before dawn some mornings. Xuan was intrigued by the girls, as a naturalist would be by some rare specimen of bird, but she could not figure out how to get closer to them. She left a box of sweets from Saigon—one of her few wedding presents—out on the kitchen table, but they were never touched. The handful of times she caught them and tried to strike up conversation, they would only stare at her with empty blue eyes before fleeing. Xuan knew three and a half different languages, but she could not understand the girls. Nhi and Vi could barely read, and were unhindered by any sense of morality or responsibility. They knew other things instead: how to shinny up a palm tree with a knife clenched between the teeth, where to go to swim without worry of leeches, what to say to make even the briniest of fishermen blush. But they did not know what to make of Xuan, either. They could not comprehend what she was doing there, living in their house, leaving her books on the table where the ancestral altar had once been, lying in wait in the kitchen to ask them questions about what they did and where they went. But they did not like or dislike her yet, so they just watched her. The eyes were everywhere in the yellow house: Old Vu watched Xuan who watched the girls who watched her, and from a distance, leaning against the fence of her chicken coop, Mrs. Dang watched them all.

IT HAD BEEN three months since the wedding. Xuan still wasn't used to her new role as Old Vu's wife and Nhi and Vi's mother, and still didn't feel that she was fulfilling it. She didn't regret it quite yet, but she was beginning to question her decision to leave her hometown to marry a man nearly fifteen years her senior. She had done it because she was lonely, but here, in the yellow house, she felt more isolated than ever.

Perhaps this was why Xuan felt strangely reassured when she began hearing voices from the bamboo grove. It meant that she was not alone. Having grown unchecked for years, the grove had become sprawling and almost impenetrable, devouring the land. When Xuan began to hear the sounds, she knew instinctively that they were coming from that darkness at the far end of the lawn. At first it was faint and wordless, whispering to her as she and Old Vu lay in bed at night with their backs to each other. She started leaving the bedroom window open, telling her husband it was because the breeze helped her sleep, when really all she wanted was to listen to the murmurs. Then one afternoon, when she was hanging out the laundry in the yard, it finally became clear; the wind rustled the bamboo and she heard her name, *Xuan, Xuan,* the soft chanting of a hundred voices, over and over. They were calling for her.

Another woman might have run back inside the house in fear, but not Xuan. She had no fear. She had read Plato and Aquinas and Descartes. She walked straight into the bamboo. "Who's there?" she called out, picking her way through the thick forest of stems.

"Xuan," the voices replied simply. "Xuan."

They became quiet when she was deep in the thicket and everything was in cool green shadow. Xuan waited but they did not speak again. She turned to make her way back out again, but suddenly she tripped over something—an old glass bottle, almost invisible in the shade—and she had to clutch wildly at the stems around her to stay upright. They shook, but she regained her footing. Several small birds, spooked by the commotion, shot out of the bamboo and flapped away noisily. Xuan tilted her head back and watched them become specks against the sky. And then she saw it fluttering down toward her between the branches. Like the birds, it, too, had been shaken loose from its bamboo perch. She caught it in her fingers: a piece of silk, tattered and filthy, now worn down to a square the size of a piece of parchment, but still as red as a fresh knife wound, and fine as a tongue of flame.

Xuan had been given less than her fair share of loveliness

in this lifetime, and so she held on tightly to this delicate cloth that had fallen into her possession. She carried it out of the bamboo and held it up to the light.

Nhi and Vi lay on their bellies on the edge of the roof, watching. When they saw the red shadow the silk cast across her face, their mouths formed identical hard lines, and they reached for each other's hand.

SISTER EMMANUEL'S VOICE trailed off. Without warning, she pulled her hands out of the mixing bowl and pushed it away from her violently. I handed her a dishcloth but as her fingers closed around it she began to shake, and the cloth fell to the kitchen floor. I dropped down to retrieve it for her. But I did not get up immediately; it was only there—kneeling at her feet, squeezing the cloth in my clammy hands that would not keep still, my face averted—that I was brave enough to ask her: "Which one are you?"

Sister Emmanuel was still shaking. "Not yet," she said. "Tomorrow."

XUAN HEARD THE VOICES even when she was away from the house. They still called out her name from time to time, but now they mostly sang her a song, always the same one. It was a simple song, made up of four notes and a handful of repeated words, but Xuan practiced it relentlessly even when the voices were quiet.

"*Chim, chim, I will find you. Chim, I will find you,*" she sang alone in the kitchen. She could see the bamboo through the window but at the moment it was silent. Her left eye was itchy, so she rubbed it with one of the ends of the red cloth that she wore tied loosely around her throat. "*Chim, I will find you, and you will be mine. Chim, chim, I will find you—*" She stopped and rubbed her eye with the cloth again.

When the silk wasn't around her neck she wore it in her hair or had it folded up and tucked secretly in between her breasts. When she lay in bed at night, she would fall asleep twisting it between her fingers while Old Vu snored beside her and had nightmares about his dead wife. She had to be touching it at all times.

The twins had begun keeping their distance from their stepmother, but they still needed to eat. They would alternate between which one had to sneak into the yellow house to scavenge for leftovers and raid the money jar. One muggy summer afternoon, while they were perched in their usual tree and their stomachs began to growl, it was Nhi's turn.

It was so oppressively hot that any sane person should have been napping; Nhi was certain she would not be seen. But just to be safe, when she left Vi in the tree and set off for home she went by the forest instead of by the road. This route concealed her from whatever eyes might have been watching, but it also forced her to walk through the bamboo grove.

Nhi entered the green thicket. Though she was so thin she could weave through the bamboo stalks without disturbing them, above her the long, tapered leaves began to move. It didn't occur to Nhi that it couldn't have been the wind, for there was none that day—the air was heavy and damp and still. The noise of the thousands of leaves brushing against one another was maddeningly loud, and because of it, Nhi did not hear the sound of Xuan singing inside the house. It was the usual tune, but this time the words were slightly different:

"*Chim, chim, I will feed you. Chim, I will feed you, and you will be mine.*"

Nhi didn't notice it until she had already climbed into the house through the window of her mother's bedroom. A photograph of Old Vu and Xuan's wedding was hanging on the wall, conveniently covering an old bloodstain. The twins were not in it. When Nhi heard the singing she cocked her head to listen, but the noise of the bamboo leaves was still muffling everything, subtle but relentless, like the sound of waves, and she could not make out the words. Curious but suspicious, she dropped to all fours and moved silently toward the kitchen.

The words were still unclear but now Nhi could hear pots and pans being moved around. As she crept into the room she saw that Xuan was preparing something by the gas stove and crooning her strange melody—the words lost in the clanging of cookware—with her back to the doorway. The jar of money was in the corner, and Nhi would have to act fast if she didn't want her stepmother to catch her. She was considering her next move when Xuan suddenly stopped singing. Outside, the leaves of the bamboo went limp and quiet once more. Without turning around, Xuan spoke sternly. "Nhi, stop behaving like an animal and stand up."

Nhi was so startled that she obeyed her stepmother instantly.

"That's better," said Xuan, still keeping her back to the girl. She lit the stove and the flame leapt to life. After a few seconds the kitchen was filled with the scent of oil warming. Nhi knew she should just bolt out the door or the window, for she was frightened, but she was also angry—seething at herself for submitting to an order, and even more furious with her stepmother for giving it. She chose not to run because she wanted to punish the woman.

Xuan, meanwhile, had dropped something into the hot oil and it was beginning to sizzle. Nhi wasn't sure what was cooking, but her stomach growled. She made a fist and ground it into her abdomen to make it stop.

Xuan had heard, though, and she giggled over by the stove. Giggling did not suit her; it was an unnatural sound. "Sit down, child," she said. "It will be done soon."

Nhi took a seat at the table without protest; her attention was now focused on the red silk looped around her stepmother's neck. It was tied in a simple overhand knot, and Xuan had thrown the ends of it over her shoulders to keep them out of the way. Nhi coolly considered walking over and shoving Xuan's face into the pot of hot oil, imagined the sound her skin would make as it fried, how the red silk would dangle into the gas flame below the pot and ignite. Then she rejected the idea—she didn't want to burn herself. Xuan had finished cooking and was now removing little morsels from the oil and putting them onto a dish. Nhi eyed the ends of the red scarf again. The silk looked strong, as if it could be pulled *very* tightly and not break, she thought with a sly smile.

"Naughty child," said Xuan, as if she could perceive her stepdaughter's violent thoughts. "Stop that. It's time to eat." She picked up the loaded plate and two sets of chopsticks; then she finally turned around.

Nhi noticed at once that something was wrong with Xuan's eye. The left one. When she sat down across from her at the table, Nhi could see that it was bloodshot and watery, the veins visible, the pupil strangely dilated. The right one, however, appeared normal. Nhi didn't want to look at her anymore. She turned her attention instead to the plate that Xuan had set down between them, piled with hot egg rolls. They were perfect cylinders, each the same size and hue. A golden pool of oil was collecting beneath them.

"Beautiful, aren't they?" said Xuan. "My mother taught me the recipe when I was a girl. I learned how to shape them with her hands around mine." She lifted her scarf up to her eye and began scrubbing at it roughly. Nhi watched the red silk move and her fingers tightened into a fist. Xuan continued speaking while she rubbed, the fabric concealing most of her face. "But I haven't made them in years; I thought I was better than this." She gestured toward the rolls with her free hand. The hand that still held the cloth to her eye was moving in quick little circles, like she was trying to wash a stubborn spot clean. "Better than cooking and kitchens. Better than husbands. Better than my own mother. I used to believe that I was too clever for that world." Her hand stopped moving. "But now I have a daughter of my own, and she will not make my mistakes." With this, she allowed the red silk to fall away from her face.

There was now a droplet of blood in the outer corner of the eye. Nhi watched with fascination as it quivered but did not fall.

"Don't you see? This is our place. We are the children of tradition. We must learn what we are taught, and then repeat it. Let me teach you, Nhi." Xuan placed one of the pairs of chopsticks on the table before the girl.

Nhi unclenched her fist to take them, and saw the crimson edges of Xuan's eye twitch. The droplet in the corner jiggled. Nhi imagined leaping out of her seat and sinking the chopsticks deep into the socket. In the distance, the leaves of the bamboo began to rustle again. She thought of her sister waiting alone in the tree, and raised her hand slowly.

"Yes. Yes, that's it," said Xuan, pushing the plate toward her. "This is our inheritance; take a bite." She smiled, and the motion finally squeezed out the tear of blood. It left a thin red trail on her cheek.

Nhi hesitated for only a moment, then brought the chopsticks plunging down.

SISTER EMMANUEL WAS SILENT. Our own egg rolls rested, complete, on the table; our mixing bowls were empty. I had been hiding my hands in my lap so she wouldn't see the way they were still moving. "You can't stop there!" I cried out. "What did she do?"

Sister Emmanuel gathered up the dirty dishes and brought them over to the sink, refusing to look at me. But I would not give up. "It can't end like that! Tell me how it really ends!" I yelled, forgetting the convent walls that surrounded us, the peace I was disturbing. "Tell me! I must know!"

Sister Emmanuel still said nothing. She simply turned to face me and then lowered her sunglasses.

By morning Sister Emmanuel had disappeared from the convent, without—as investigation later proved—taking anything with her. There was some initial disquiet when word got out, but the affair was mostly hushed up. After a few months she was never even spoken of, as if the very memory of her had vanished from this place. But how could I forget? I, who had lost both my faith and the only person on earth who knew my apostasy.

Some of the other sisters did worry when my shaking began occurring too regularly to hide, and voiced their concerns to Mother Superior. Eventually the abbess called me into her office and advised me to go see a doctor about the "trouble with my hands." She was terribly confused when I tried to explain to her that the real problem was not with my hands but my vision.

"But your eyes are fine, dear girl!" she insisted.

"My eyes work perfectly, but I cannot see the way I used to," I replied.

"You mean that you are going blind?"

"Precisely the opposite, Mother Superior. I see too much."

She sighed, and dismissed me.

I've since learned that the only way I can stop the shaking is to retreat to the kitchen and make egg rolls. My hands remember how. It keeps the parish soup kitchen well stocked, which perhaps is the story's happy ending. Sometimes I even sing while I work.

GUESTS

—

Mia worked in the immigrations department of the U.S. Consulate in Ho Chi Minh City, filing visas and dual-citizenship requests for pre-'76 Amerasians and younger mothers claiming that their child had been fathered by an American. It wasn't the kind of career that Mia's parents had anticipated for their daughter. She'd had a happy, healthy suburban childhood, she'd been the president of her sorority chapter, she'd even interned on Capitol Hill. She was supposed to go far professionally, not geographically. Mia told her parents that she had taken the job for the adventure, but her father, while not a particularly superstitious man, could never quite rid himself of the belief that because he had escaped Vietnam in 1973 with his life—albeit with a bullet in the left leg and damage to both eardrums—the powers of the universe had lured his only child to that godawful country thirty years later in some sort of karmic trade-off.

He never told Mia his theory, and Mia never admitted her irrational fear to her father that one day an unexpected, older Vietnamese half sibling would turn up at her office.

The mothers rarely had verification of the child's paternity. Mia would ask them, exasperated, for any proof, for anything at all. Just a photograph of the alleged father would be sufficient to get the paperwork and interview process started, but sometimes they didn't even know his name. They would point out the paleness of the baby's skin, or the straightness of its nose, and seem surprised that Mia needed to know anything further.

"I swear, I would have studied genetics instead of poli sci if I'd known the job would be like this," she said to her boyfriend Charlie one Saturday afternoon. The air-conditioning was broken in the apartment again, so they were both lying on the kitchen tile in their underwear. Charlie was too long to fit all of himself on the kitchen floor, so his legs were actually in the living room. It was too hot to even think about having sex. Mia licked her lips and continued. "Sometimes I feel like one of those Hitler-doctors from the thirties, you know? The eugenics scientists who measured people's skulls to test whether they were Aryan or whatever? That's all I can think about when somebody hands their kid to me and says, 'It's half American! Just look at it! Look at what color it is!' Best-case scenario is when the dad's black—makes it a lot easier to prove."

"That's terrible," said Charlie, and Mia didn't know whether he meant that her last statement had been terrible, that she was terrible for comparing herself to a Nazi, or that her situation was terrible. She didn't pursue clarification. It was too hot for that, too.

Charlie taught English at the Australian International University even though he was American. If he ever worried about color it was over whether or not he should spell it with a *u*.

Mia had only been in Ho Chi Minh City for two months when she met him at a Lunar New Year celebration in the park. Even in the frenetic whorl of firecrackers and screaming children and leaping lion dancers that night, they spotted each other—two freckled, blond beings obviously far from home. Mia fell into Charlie's circle quickly. His friends were all foreign and therefore transient: They were English teachers and backpackers who had gotten sidetracked and lingered, they worked at embassies and nonprofits, they always left eventually. They had all arrived in Vietnam telling themselves that it was only temporary yet wanting more than anything to fit in. They thought their old lives were something that could be husked, but when it became apparent that they were not, they sought out the comforts of home together: American fast food and French bakeries and Italian coffee. The group shrank when members left in search of other jobs, to start families, to find somewhere to live that was quieter and had better weather, but fresh expats always came along to fill their places.

On any given night of the week they could be found drunk in a spectacularly public fashion around the bars of District 1. Mia and the girls tottered down the street in stilettos that were not engineered for crooked Vietnamese pavement, and Charlie and the boys wore their old rugby jerseys and drank as much liquor as they wanted because it was cheap. After the bars closed they bought Saigon Beer from twenty-four-hour convenience stores and drank on the sidewalk like locals, the girls perched on the laps of the boys because they wouldn't sit on the ground. If men lurking on motorbikes heckled them from the shadows, the boys would throw their empty cans at them until they stopped. At the end of the night they stuffed seven people into one taxi because they had spent all their money on cocktails. It was the only way they knew how to entertain themselves here.

After six months of primarily intoxicated dates, Charlie moved out of his boardinghouse in District 2 and into Mia's consulate-provided apartment with unreliable electricity. He didn't have much, even though he had been in Vietnam a year longer than Mia: one box of books, one bag of clothes, his computer, and a large ceramic bust of Ho Chi Minh with a broken ear that he had fished out of a trash can on a whim and grown attached to. He managed to move everything over to her place in a single motorbike trip—the book box between his knees, Mia on the seat behind him with Broken-Ear Uncle Ho cradled in her arms, and the bag with his clothes and laptop between them. But though he lacked material possessions Charlie wasn't hard up for cash, nor was he a "hippie-dippy love-child commie apologist," which was what Mia's father would have called him had he known Charlie existed. Charlie just didn't accumulate things. Mia, on the other hand, did not travel light. She had arrived in Ho Chi Minh City with three suitcases of clothes alone, but half the items were impractical for the heat and the other half didn't fit her after the first month because she wouldn't eat Vietnamese food and her weight plummeted. It was Charlie who took her to get her clothes tailored and coaxed her to eat at restaurants she would have never gone into by herself and persuaded her to sign up for a language course even if he couldn't make her practice.

He was good to her, but he wasn't perfect. Mia looked over at his lanky body next to hers, sprawled belly-up in a pair of checkered boxers. His face and forearms and lower legs were tanned gold, but the rest of him was pale, splotched pink in places from the heat. He was the color of some sort of Italian dessert, she thought. Mia was very aware of the fact that Charlie had had relationships with several of the female Vietnamese teachers at his school, and at least once with an older student. Everyone in their circle knew, and Charlie had never tried to hide it from her. She remembered going out for ice cream on one of their early dates and seeing Charlie's face suddenly freeze in horror, mid-lick.

"What's wrong?" Mia had asked, and turned, following his gaze, to see a Vietnamese girl, young (but they all looked so young—even the middle-aged ones—didn't they?) and quite beautiful, with a waterfall of dark hair, looking at Charlie with tragic eyes from across the room. He had hustled Mia out of the café promptly.

"An ex," he explained. "A crazy one." She had worked in his foreign language department, he told Mia, and used to practice her English with him. She was cute and had seemed like a normal girl. A modern girl. They would go out together for drinks and karaoke and it was fun at first. "But after we slept together once she just assumed I was going to marry her," he said flatly. He had been honest with her—other guys would have played along for the sex and then dumped her later on, he said. But Charlie told her straight out that he wasn't looking for a wife and gently suggested that they break it off, since they wanted different things. "And then she went completely insane!" he said. "She scratched my face up and stormed off, but then for months afterward she kept calling me and showing up at my place, banging on the door and screaming how much she hated me or how much she loved me. It was scary. I don't want her to jump you with a knife or something. Not that I think she really would," he had added quickly, seeing Mia's face.

According to their male expat friends, most of whom had been with a local girl at one point or another, all Vietnamese women were unstable and prone to fits of jealous rage. "Which means that you've got a whole horde of angry Asian ladies in this city to watch out for," one had jokingly warned Mia on some drunken night, before Charlie nudged him in the ribs and he fell silent. When Charlie first found out what Mia's job was, he had sworn to her, unprompted, that he had used a condom with each of his Vietnamese girlfriends, no exceptions. But that didn't stop her from scrutinizing the face of each half-Asian infant that was thrust upon her; from looking, despite herself, for the features that she knew well.

———

CHARLIE GROANED ON THE kitchen floor. "Too. Hot."

"I have a sweat puddle underneath me," said Mia.

"I have a sweat lagoon."

"Cold shower?"

"By the time we dry off we'll just be sweating again."

"Then where can we find air-conditioning?"

"Free air-conditioning or air-conditioning with a price?"

"I don't care how much it costs. I would sell my soul for a breeze."

"Movies then. Best air-conditioning in all of Southeast Asia."

Charlie drove them on his secondhand motorbike, snaking through traffic and speeding down the wider streets to create wind for her. Mia still didn't know how to handle a bike; Charlie's last attempt at driving lessons had left her with cuts up and down her arms and raw knees. They got tickets to a movie that had come out back home three months earlier and bought Vietnamese popcorn that they both agreed was terrible. In the blessedly cool dark of the theater, Mia rested her head on Charlie's shoulder and wondered if his other girlfriends had ever done the same or if they had all been too short to reach.

ON MONDAY MORNINGS CHARLIE taught early and needed to leave the apartment by 6:45, but he could rarely get himself out of bed before 6:30. It was Mia who woke up, fumbled around for the off-switch on the alarm clock, and picked out a clean pair of slacks, button-up, and necktie from the dresser. She laid them out on the bed, then went into the kitchen to start coffee in the expensive machine she had purchased despite Charlie's protests that she could buy a cup of Vietnamese *cà phê* on literally any street corner for about fifty cents. It wasn't about the money for Mia, or even the taste— what she needed was the routine of measuring the grounds, of listening to the coffee gurgle, and timing herself to make Charlie's sandwich before it finished brewing. If the process was disrupted it would spoil the rest of her day.

As she was opening the refrigerator, Mia heard a pathetic mewling from the kitchen window. The neighborhood's resident stray cat had climbed up the drainpipe again and was trying to get in. It was a wormy-looking tabby with bald patches in its coat and half its tail gone, and Mia hated it.

"Hey!" she yelled. "Go away!" It had no effect on the cat, who just whined again and pawed at the windowpane, but the noise had successfully awakened Charlie. Mia heard him making low, muffled, morning groans into his pillow, and a few moments later his footfall on the way to the bathroom. She turned her attention back to the cat and was repulsed to see that it was now standing upright on the ledge, balancing on its two hind legs and scrabbling at the window with its forefeet. Its head was perfectly level with hers. "Hey!" She slapped the glass repeatedly. The cat wasn't usually this persistent. Mia had to resort to banging with both fists before it finally gave up and lowered itself back onto all fours. But before skulking away, the creature stared at Mia through the window for a long moment, its yellow-green eyes unblinking. Then, as if it knew the reaction it would provoke and relished it, the cat slowly leaned forward and pressed its nose against the pane with a dull, rubbery sound. Mia shuddered.

The coffee machine beeped gently to signal that it had finished brewing, and Mia flicked her eyes over to the yet-unassembled sandwich ingredients on the counter. When she looked back at the window the cat was gone.

After she had seen Charlie out the door, Mia lingered over her coffee. She showered and then wandered around the apartment in her towel, her hair in a wet tangle that dripped onto the carpet. Their landlord had fixed the air-conditioning on Sunday, and before leaving for work Mia stood in front of the vent for five minutes to try to soak up as much of the cold as she could. It didn't work—she started sweating the moment she stepped out the door.

Mia viewed her walk to the consulate as a video game where the goal was to make it to work without accidentally touching anything, or having anyone touch her. In Ho Chi Minh City everything spilled into everything else or was stacked on top of it, and Mia could barely go a step without almost tripping over a fruit stand or a noodle cart or a sleeping dog or a sleeping homeless person. Even on the sidewalks she was in danger of being run over by a motorbike because traffic didn't stay in the roads. There was no concept of personal space, either. Strangers would come up to Mia in public and tug at her blond hair, pinch her pale skin, even follow her home, just because she was so obviously, obtrusively *foreign*. Her very physical presence in their country was baffling. Here, the people were small, quick, and compact, able to maneuver the clutter and crooked corners of their world. Mia was too gangly, too loose of limb. She simply did not fit.

This was proven anew to her when she reached the office. Mia knocked an elbow on the door frame coming in, and when she jerked away in pain, she hit her thigh on the corner of a desk. There were three desks in the room even though only Mia worked in it; she didn't know to whom the other two desks belonged, why they had been deposited in her office, or why her requests to have them removed went unmet. Her co-workers on the third floor didn't know, either, but didn't mind because they used the mystery desks and the area around them as a place to dump extra paperwork and odds and ends that wouldn't fit in their own, cramped offices. Today she was shar-ing the room with two new chairs, a broken lamp, a stack of crates, and somebody's rice cooker. She checked that she was alone, then hiked up her skirt and crawled under her desk to get to her chair, because it seemed like less effort than the gym-nastics required to go around it.

Mia kept a framed photograph of Charlie on the window-sill, but when she had appointments with the mothers she would hide him in a desk, then put him back up after they were gone. She both liked and did not like it when her female Vietnamese co-workers saw his picture and told Mia how handsome he was.

This morning she needed to finish typing up statements made by Nguyen Thi Thanh Ha, age twenty-eight, Vo Thi Ly Huong, age forty-one, and Phan Thi Thu Trang, age nineteen. She did the second case first so she could get it over with and forget about it quickly. Ms. Huong, according to her story, was supposed to be the mail-order bride of a wealthy, older American. He had flown over to meet her, stayed for three days, and in that time got her pregnant. He returned home and then, months later, as the translator put it, "canceled the trans-action" with Ms. Huong. Desperate, Ms. Huong had tried canceling the product of the transaction that was now grow-ing in her womb, but instead of going to a doctor she sought out the help of a healer in her neighborhood. The concoction of herbs that Ms. Huong drank did not terminate the preg-nancy, but did—she discovered after giving birth—hideously deform the child. When Ms. Huong had first brought her baby to the consulate to make her claim, Mia hadn't been able to resist the urge to recoil from it. She still felt guilty. Mia didn't know why Ms. Huong thought that American citizenship would help the twisted, drooling infant in her arms, but it wasn't her job to worry about things like that. She only lis-tened, took careful notes, and asked questions, and then typed it all up later. Before she left the office, Ms. Huong had placed the child on Mia's desk and gestured at it, saying something in rapid Vietnamese.

"It's the hair," the translator told Mia. "She wants you to look at the hair." The child's head—though too long for its body and misshapen, and with a lower jaw that could not close—was covered in soft, dark hair. Not straight, black, and coarse, like its mother's, but fine, with a slight curl to it and a color that changed to polished chestnut when the sunlight hit it. "She says that even though the baby is wrong, it has beautiful hair."

DURING HER LUNCH BREAK, Mia went out for a manicure. She had been avoiding it for almost two weeks but couldn't put it off any longer. If her nails weren't done she ended up chewing them off or picking at her cuticles until they bled. Mia hated that she couldn't get rid of the habit and had sworn to herself that she would never let Charlie discover it.

The nail salon was only a few minutes' walk from the consulate, but to get there she had to first pass the motorbike repair shop. Mia smelled the shop before she could see it—the ripe mix of rust and oil and tire rubber in the sun—and her pulse quickened as she approached. She tried to hide her face with her hair before remembering that her hair was arguably an even more distinguishing foreign feature than her face. It didn't matter in any case, because he had already spotted her.

"Mia! My Mia!" Tuan was leaning on a partially assembled yellow Honda. He wore a pair of low-slung, cutoff fatigues, and his hands and forearms were streaked black with axle grease. "Finally you come to see me!" he called out languidly.

Mia knew she should just hurry past without a word like she did most of the time, but she could feel the way her blouse was sticking to her back and for some reason couldn't bear the thought of him staring after her enormous sweat patch as she walked away. She stood facing the shop from the street, unable to move.

Mia saw Tuan's face light up once he realized that she was stopping. He checked his reflection quickly in the Honda's side mirror before sauntering out to meet her. The other greasy, shirtless workers looked up from their motorbike parts and grinned or waggled their eyebrows at him as he passed.

"Hi, Tuan," Mia said evenly. He was tall for a Vietnamese man, but they were still exactly the same height.

"My Mia." Tuan tacked on the possessive so casually that she barely noticed. "Why you do not call me?" He had given her his number four different times during their fleeting lunch break interactions (she would not let herself call them flirtations) and pressed her regularly to go out with him for dinner, coffee, Vietnamese lessons, and occasionally the euphemistic-sounding "getting to know you specially."

"I'm sorry," said Mia, which was not an answer.

"Perhaps you lost?" he asked with a half smile. Mia wasn't sure if he was being purposefully cryptic or if it was just his English.

She couldn't think of anything else to say, and he stayed silent, too. For half a minute they stood there quietly, only about a foot apart, simply observing each other. Was this normal here? Should it feel wrong? Mia didn't know. Miraculously, she had stopped sweating, but she could guess how clammy and pink her face still was. Tuan's face was deeply tanned, and broad and gently sloped in the places where hers was sharply angled. Looking at him was like looking into a mirror that, instead of her reflection, presented the image of her exact physical counter. His eyes were narrow and dark and reminded Mia of tadpoles, which wouldn't sound like a compliment, even if it was.

Without speaking, Tuan reached into his pocket. The movement took Mia by surprise; in her mind she had still been imagining him as her reflection, so it was a shock when he moved without her. He pulled out a faded receipt and a stubby pencil. Though both were already dirty, he wiped his hands off on his shorts and wrote with the pencil held lightly between his thumb and third finger because they were the least greasy. When he was finished, he offered the receipt to Mia and she took it from him without letting their skin touch. She slipped it into her handbag without looking at the ten digits scrawled across the top; she already knew that he wrote his ones the way she wrote her sevens, and he wrote his sevens the European way, with a little dash in the middle of their stem.

"You will call me," said Tuan. His voice was teasing, but there was something pleasantly chilling in his words. Prophetic, almost. Mia didn't want to leave, which made it all the more imperative that she did. But before drawing away from him, Mia (though to her it felt like her body was acting of its own accord) raised a finger—pale and thin, the nail peeking out through its chipped polish—up to his face and gently closed his eyelids, the left first, then the right.

"Don't move," she said each time. "Don't move." She

wasn't sure what reaction she had been expecting from him. Shock, perhaps. Confusion. Discomfort. But Tuan calmly accepted her touch. It almost seemed as if he expected it. He did not open his eyes once she had shut them, but she felt them tremble beneath her finger. It was like touching a butterfly wing. Mia took a step back. She wasn't quite sure what she had just done. The other workers inside the shop were calling something out to her but all she heard in her head was buzzing. Tuan remained motionless. Mia wondered if this was what he looked like while he slept. Then she broke away and hurried away down the street. Before turning the corner she looked back. Even in the painfully bright midday sun, she could tell that his eyes were still closed.

Inside the nail salon, the powerful smell of acetone washed away whatever madness had possessed Mia. She would not think about Tuan. She would walk the long way back to the consulate so she wouldn't pass the motorbike shop. After work she would go to the market and buy vegetables for dinner. Mia selected a pale, pinky-gold bottle that she had used before and handed it to the manicurist.

"Hmm. Pretty color," the woman said.

SHOPPING AT THE LOCAL market was always a stressful event for Mia, but there was no logical reason to go to the large, Western grocery store on the far side of town for produce when she could buy it around the corner. Charlie liked the fray of the marketplace for some reason. He even liked the way it smelled, calling it "pungent," which really meant that it stunk of dead things and pickled things and dirty hands touching dirty food. He didn't mind when he stepped in puddles that could have been water or could have been fish juices. He enjoyed haggling over prices with the old, pajama-clad ladies, and he just laughed when giant rats ran across the top of the butcher's stand in plain sight. But going to the market made Mia feel almost physically ill.

Clenching her teeth, she ducked down and entered the shantytown of tarp-covered stalls. Immediately, it felt about ten degrees hotter. Here space was even harder to come by than on the street. Mia had to hunch to avoid hitting her head on the tarps above, which sagged with rainwater, and navigated the stalls and towers of precariously balanced produce like she was picking her way through a minefield. The paths through the market were less than a foot across, but this did not discourage the Vietnamese from trying to drive their motorbikes down it. But what Mia loathed most was that everyone stared at her: the white woman who had crossed into this most sacred of cultural spaces. Temples and pagodas she could explore at her leisure without a second glance. Those were the places where tourists were supposed to be. But here, Mia felt all their eyes on her. The eyes of the vendors, the eyes of the people buying from them, and also the glassy eyes of the fish in their baskets, the eyes of dead chickens hanging upside down from hooks, the eyes of the still-live frogs in plastic tubs waiting to be skinned.

The ladies who sold vegetables started cackling to each

other when they saw Mia approaching their stalls. "Hel-loooooo! Madame, you buy from meeeee?" they crooned, and then giggled themselves silly.

Mia pointed to the carrots and held up three fingers. "Okayokayokay!" said one of the ladies, the one who always wore the same polka-dotted pajama set. While she put the carrots into the bag Mia pointed to the tomatoes and held up five fingers.

The lady with a large mole on her neck grinned. "Five!" she said, and put them in another bag. "Wan too ta-ree fo five!"

"You can put them with the carrots," said Mia before she could stop herself.

"Yes?" said Polka-Dotted Pajamas.

"The same bag. You can put . . . in there? Together?" Mia made a halfhearted attempt at an explanatory gesture.

"Yes!" said Neck-Mole, and then she and Polka-Dotted Pajamas burst out laughing again and tied the bags closed.

"Fifteen thousand Vietnam dollar!" they shouted in unison between cackles. Mia pulled one ten-thousand and five one-thousand crinkled bills from her wallet and counted them carefully; in the past she had accidentally confused hundred-thousand bills for ten-thousand ones. She really didn't see why Vietnamese currency operated in such big figures in the first place. Fifteen thousand was about seventy-five cents. When Mia was handing over the money, Neck-Mole leaned over the vegetables and grabbed a lock of her hair. As she waited for the woman to lose interest and stop stroking, Mia imagined that this must be how dogs who lived in households with small children felt all the time. Neck-Mole finally released her and Mia turned, hunched down, and fled directly into the path of a motorbike roaring up behind her.

The hot pink Yamaha beeped furiously but did not stop. Mia darted back in time to avoid being hit, but the bike's tailpipe brushed the side of her leg, searing the skin instantly. The tears welled up before she could control them, and she dropped her bag of tomatoes. Her vision was blurry but she could see the driver—a very long, dark ponytail hanging down her back—weave around a pile of cucumbers and disappear into the maze of stalls.

Mia wiped her eyes and began gathering the scattered tomatoes. None of the vegetable ladies were laughing at her now.

THE COIN-SIZED BURN MARK was a dark red color by the time she made it back to the apartment. Mia hadn't thought that her day could get any worse, but waiting outside to greet her, lurking by the trash cans on the corner, was the hideous cat.

"Why hasn't someone eaten you yet?!" she yelled at it.

The tabby gave one of its pitiful yowls and tottered toward her. Mia could see that the thing was limping now. She hoped it was because it had fallen off the drainpipe. That would discourage it from climbing. Mia ran to the door, wedged herself through, and slammed it shut behind her.

Charlie was by the stove, boiling water for pasta. Mia

dumped the carrots and the bruised tomatoes on the counter and tried to respond with some enthusiasm to the kiss he greeted her with, but couldn't manage much.

"Mmm . . . long day?" Charlie asked and patted Mia's head absently. "Hey! What was that?" His hand on her hair had made her flinch. "Am I that disgusting?"

Mia forced a laugh and nibbled his ear in what she hoped was a convincingly playful manner, then escaped to the bathroom to find some burn cream and a bandage for her leg. While she was alone, she took the grubby receipt from her handbag and tucked it into the enamel box that held her jewelry, a bottle of perfume that her parents had mailed her for Christmas, and four other receipts, each with the same ten digits written across the top in pencil, all of the sevens crossed. Mia returned to the kitchen, fished a knife from the drawer, and reached for the carrots but had the sudden urge to seize all her blond hair in a fist and start chopping at that instead.

Charlie's phone buzzed while they were eating. "The people want to go out," he said to her after he had finished reading the message. "Pub or club?"

" 'The People'? How very Socialist Republic of you," Mia said, half to herself. She rose from the table and took her mostly untouched plate into the kitchen.

"Pub or club?" repeated Charlie louder from the living room table, not to be deterred.

"Pub. Don't you have your early class tomorrow?" Mia was over by the window, scanning the sides of the building and the street below for any sign of the cat.

Charlie didn't answer because he had lifted his plate up to his mouth and was shoveling in the rest of his dinner. When it was empty he brought it into the kitchen and dropped it into the sink. "I'll wash up later," he said, giving her a little smack on the rear. "Go get your shoes on."

Before they left, Mia checked the window twice to make sure that it was locked.

THEIR FAVORITE BAR had changed ownership four times during the year and a half that Mia had been in Vietnam. Its name had switched, too, from the Tiger Cage to B52 Bar to the Hairy Guerrilla and then back to the Tiger Cage, but the interior always remained the same. The back wall was taken up by a lovingly rendered mural of Marx, Lenin, and Ho Chi Minh frolicking together in a swimming-pool–sized bowl of *phở*. Marx was wearing water wings and a snorkel. The remaining walls were covered in the graffiti of permanent-marker–wielding patrons: names, phone numbers, vulgar doodles of an anatomical nature, poetry and profanity in English, Vietnamese, French, German, and at least ten other languages. The tables arranged haphazardly around the room were long and low, and everybody sat on cushions on the hardwood floor, but somebody's architectural miscalculation had resulted in the bar itself being absurdly high. The bartenders stood on crates behind it, and even Mia had to crane a bit when she ordered drinks—she would never admit it, but this usually factored into her decision to wear heels. The Tiger Cage's most striking feature was the chandelier at its center, constructed from barbed wire, naked lightbulbs, and empty gin bottles. Charlie and his friends had wandered in by drunken accident one night, looking for a different bar down a different dark alley, and liked the light fixture so much that they ended up staying.

When they entered the Tiger Cage, heads turned, but Mia didn't mind these stares because no one was just looking at her, or at Charlie, but at the couple they made. Individually they were each tall and attractive and Teutonic-looking, but together they were even more striking. They were like a pair of gods who had accidentally alighted on the wrong world, aquiline-nosed and with hair so pale it looked white.

"I swear, you two emit fucking *light*!" said Charlie's friend Neil, standing to welcome the two of them when they reached the table. Neil gave Charlie a sloppy hug/backslap and squeezed Mia on her side, right on her little handle of hip fat. Mia didn't know why he thought this was an appropriate way to greet his friend's girlfriend, but Neil was Canadian and perhaps this sort of gesture was more acceptable there. Tonight the usual crew was assembled, but there was also a new face among them. A pretty Vietnamese one. The girl was wearing a very complicated blouse that was simultaneously high-necked, short-sleeved, ruffled, and cleavage-revealing, accompanied by a pair of microscopic shorts.

"Introductions!" said Neil. It was clear that he had been imbibing for at least an hour already. "Mia, this is my little friend Barry. Barry, this is the lovely Mia, and you already know Charlie."

Mia looked from Neil to Charlie to the girl, then back to Charlie. "Oh, really?" she said. There was a hot, squirmy pain in her gut. Barry stood. She came up to Mia's shoulder in her platform sandals, the straps of which were—Mia noticed grimly—also ruffled.

"I am Strawberry," the girl said, and beamed broadly, revealing an impressive set of crooked, brown, tombstone-shaped teeth. She had difficulty pronouncing most of the consonants in her name, and Mia gathered that this was why she had become "Barry."

"Did you pick that out yourself?" asked Mia.

Charlie cut her a side-eye. "Don't condescend," he warned softly. But Barry hadn't noticed; it was unclear whether or not she had actually understood Mia's question. The rest of their friends had automatically shifted so that Charlie could sit at the head of the table with Mia and Neil to his right and left, but Mia decided that she didn't want to be near either of them. She linked arms with Barry.

"Boys are so boring. Let's go have girl-talk," she hissed conspiratorially, and led Barry—who was wide-eyed with panic as she was steered away from Neil—to the other end of the table.

Almost immediately it was confirmed that Barry's English was almost as bad as Mia's Vietnamese. Girl-talk lasted about two minutes—"You're friends with Charlie?" "I am friend of Charlie!" "I like your shoes." "I like shoes!" "Where did you buy them?" "I buy!"—before Mia gave up and ordered tequila shots. They were followed by a gin and tonic, a glass of something pink that one of the bartenders had invented, and several Long Island iced teas, which Barry discovered she liked after Mia let her try hers. She abandoned Mia shortly after that to go sit on Neil's lap. Mia also observed that the hand she didn't have wrapped around Neil's neck was creeping in the direction of Charlie's thigh.

After drink number four, Mia started Splitting. That was how she had begun referring to it in her head. It was nothing strange: Once she had attained a certain degree of tipsiness, her consciousness underwent a kind of mitosis. She continued to chat with the girls, exchanging work grievances and gossip, pausing intermittently to cheer with the boys or partake in suggestive banter with Charlie to make their single friends jealous. But simultaneously she was watching them all, herself included, from a distance, like a pair of invisible swiveling eyeballs in the corner. This Split-Mia could see all of the tiny gestures, the glances, the twitches of lips when someone went to speak but then thought better of it, which Stuck-Mia could not. Mia had only started Splitting after coming to Vietnam, but she was sure that it must happen to plenty of other people. Still, she hadn't told anyone about it.

Tonight, while Stuck-Mia spent five minutes showing off her new manicure, Split-Mia turned her attention to a small commotion at the other end of the table. Whenever Charlie drank liquor his face turned into a beetroot, and Neil found this hilarious.

"Dude's got the Asian Flush!" he was shouting at anyone who would listen, and slapping the arms of those who wouldn't until they did. "Whiteboy caught the Asian Flush! That shit's contagious! It's an STD!" Neil dropped his head and stared at Barry's breasts. "I want your disease!" he yelled down at them. Split-Mia noticed Stuck-Mia eavesdropping. Suddenly, an uncharacteristically serious look came over Neil's face. Keeping one hand positioned on Barry's thigh meat, only partially for balance, he leaned over and spoke to Charlie in what he thought was a confidential whisper:

"I've been kind of worried about you, man."

Charlie could barely focus his eyes anymore but still managed to look cagey. "Yeah?"

"Let's face it, dude, you've turned. You've gone domestic." He waited for a protest from Charlie, and when it didn't come he continued: "Now don't take this the wrong way. I *love* Mia, you know that. She's, like, Consular Barbie and everything. But don't you miss the *freedom*?"

Charlie chewed on the cocktail straw in his whiskey-Coke but said nothing.

"Remember back in the beginning?" Neil pressed. "When we were here because we were sick of the shit we got back home? Like, rules and expectations and people asking what the hell you were planning to do with your college degree? We didn't have to give a fuck because we were in Vietnam! The food was cheap, the booze was cheap, and all the local ladies wanted to get with us. Don't you miss that? Because now you're part of this perfect couple and it feels like you two are halfway down the aisle and getting ready to make your perfect neon-blond babies and—"

The whiskey-Coke came down on the table just hard enough to cut him off, but not so forcefully that it couldn't have been called an accident. Charlie's hair was plastered to his forehead with sweat, and he had spilled his drink down the front of his shirt, but there was a reason why he was the alpha-male. "Finish up this round and then it's half-off vodka buckets at that place on De Tham Street. The one that used to be Comrade Something's Lounge. How does that sound?" This last part was addressed to Barry with a smile and received a crooked brown grin in response.

Split-Mia was the only one who saw a spasm of unchecked emotion ripple across Stuck-Mia's face, distorting her features for an instant. Then the two Mias fused together once more, and she slung back the rest of her gin and tonic.

It was just past midnight. The group loitered in the Tiger Cage's stairwell while Charlie went to the bathroom and a couple of the girls smoked. Mia leaned her back against the concrete, wondering how it could be so cool and solid when she felt so hot and throbbing and half made of liquid. She imagined sticking out a stiletto-shod foot to intercept Charlie on his way back from the bathroom. It was the sort of femme fatale-y move she would have been able to pull off in her old life, but here she would probably break his neck instead. Charlie came down the stairs, one hand on the wall to help him stay upright. "Hey," Mia called softly.

He smiled clumsily when he realized who it was and went

to put his mouth on her neck, but she caught him by the hair before he could.

"You torment me," he murmured, and licked her face instead.

"Let me go home." She had meant to say, "Let's go home," but it hadn't come out right.

Charlie planted himself with his hands on either side of Mia and his lips migrated farther up her face, past the cheekbone. "But it's so early!" he whined against her temple.

"I'm sorry," she said.

Charlie frowned suddenly. "What happened to your leg?" he asked. Then he cut her off before she could reply: "Wait a minute, I have to pee again." He fumbled back up the stairs.

Mia felt someone tugging at her elbow. "Charlie go where?" It was Barry.

"He's in the bathroom," said Mia frostily.

Barry looked blank. "I do not know."

Mia tried again. "The restroom?"

"I do not know."

"Toilet?"

"Oh! I know!" Barry nodded enthusiastically. Satisfied, she leaned against the wall next to Mia and, perhaps to pass the time, pulled out her cellphone. Mia glanced over as the screen lit up; the background was a picture of Barry with two other Vietnamese girls, all laughing, their arms thrown around one another. Barry was in the middle. The girl to her left wore thick glasses and her hair was bobbed, but the other one had hair down to her waist and looked suspiciously familiar.

Mia felt her stomach twist. "Let me see that," she said, and grabbed the phone from Barry's hand. It was a cheap thing—Chinese knockoff—and the picture was all grainy. Mia held it up to her face and studied the girl on the right. The image was too blurry for her to tell for sure whether or not it was Charlie's ex-girlfriend from the ice-cream parlor, but clear enough that Mia knew she was beautiful. "Who is this?" she asked Barry, pointing to the screen.

Barry snatched her phone back and gave Mia a look of annoyance. "My friend," she said, and walked off, the thump of her heavy sandals echoing in the stairwell.

OUTSIDE, MIA WAITED WITH the rest of the group while they hailed a cab. She helped Neil stuff the slumping Charlie into the front seat while the others played human Tetris to get everyone else into the back. Barry had come separately, on a motorbike, so Neil rode with her instead of squeezing into the taxi, too. He climbed on behind her and fastened the straps of a blue helmet. She wore a hot pink one that matched the color of the bike. When Mia saw Neil's fingers playing along the hem of Barry's shorts, she turned and left.

The moment she was back in the apartment she kicked her shoes down the corridor and sat down on the kitchen floor to massage the arches of her feet. Mia had sobered up considerably on the walk home, so it was strange when she found herself Splitting again, particularly because this was the first time it had happened while she was alone. Split-Mia hovered by the kitchen window and observed Stuck-Mia because there was no one else to watch. Stuck-Mia sat on the floor and rubbed her sore feet with her gold-tipped fingers. After a while she looked up at the window, and though she couldn't see Split-Mia, they were looking straight at each other.

At two thirty, Mia woke up when she heard Charlie in the bathroom, dropping things and cursing at the toilet and pissing noisily. Afterward he managed to get his boxers pulled up but not his jeans—he just waddled over to the bed with them in a puddle around his ankles, his belt jangling like the bell on a kitten's collar, and then passed out facedown. Mia lay blinking in the darkness for a long time before she could fall asleep again. But when she did, she dreamed about Ms. Huong's deformed baby. She was holding it in her lap and gently stroking its hair, over and over again.

When the alarm went off four hours later, Mia let it ring for five torturous minutes. Charlie was awake—Mia could hear how his breathing had changed—but he made no effort to move. Eventually she crawled over his inert body and switched the alarm off. She got up and went over to the dresser, wincing as she walked—the burn on her leg was throbbing this morning, though her head felt fine. Mia selected Charlie's work outfit for the day, and unfolded the clothes on the bed next to him. After she finished she remained by the bed, surveying Charlie's motionless mass. As if he could feel the weight of her stare, Charlie lifted his face from the pillow and scowled at her.

"Unf," he said. He hauled himself out of bed, then shed his

pants and underwear and walked naked to the shower. Mia gathered his discarded clothes, which reeked of smoke and alcohol, deposited them in the laundry basket, and went to start the coffee and make Charlie's sandwich. As soon as she stepped into the kitchen, she froze.

The window was open. The latch was dangling unfastened; balmy morning air permeated the apartment. Mia dashed across the room and slammed the window shut. She locked it, jiggled the latch to see if it was loose, and when it wasn't, she finally exhaled. But a few seconds later, her breath caught in her throat once more when she saw that the windowsill was covered in long, deep scratches. In order to make marks like that, the cat must have clawed the wood relentlessly, over and over. Horrified, Mia backed away from the window just as Charlie entered the kitchen wrapped in a towel, scrubbed and rosy and battling an imperial hangover.

He made a sound that was halfway between a groan and a grunt, and reached around Mia to get a glass of water.

Mia repositioned herself so that Charlie was between her and the window. "How was the rest of the night?" she asked brightly as she began messing about with the lunch fixings, and hoped he couldn't see her hands shaking.

Charlie shrugged and said something else in Neanderthal.

"Did you have a good time with Barry? I'm so disappointed that you've never introduced us before." Mia slathered mustard viciously on a slice of bread. "We had *such* fun talking together. She's quite the sparkling conversationalist. A real wit. An—"

"Don't do that." Charlie had regained his use of language. "It's so ugly. And Barry's a riot when you actually try and get to know her."

But Mia couldn't stop herself. "I'm sure I'll learn what a riot she is in another nine months when she and little Neil Junior show up at my office. No, wait, I guess she'd have to go over to the Canadian Consulate, wouldn't she?"

Charlie finished drinking his water and placed the glass down carefully on the counter. "I don't know why you're like this," he said. His voice was so deliciously cold. Mia shivered. "You chose to live here, did you forget that? No one forced you to come work in this country. No one held a gun up to your head and told you to stay. Why are you even in Vietnam? You hate your job. You don't have any compassion for the people here. When was the last time you actually talked to a local person who wasn't selling you something?"

Mia threw her knife into the sink, which was still full of dirty dishwater; then, as an afterthought, threw in the slice of mustard-covered bread, too. "Make your own sandwich," she said.

"I *never* asked you to make my fucking sandwiches for me," spat Charlie. "Not once. I never asked you to pick out my clothes. I never wanted you to pretend to be a—to be my *wife*. God, for someone who hates Vietnamese women, you're just like one."

"No," said Mia. "They fuck you because they think they'll get a green card out of it. I do it just because I couldn't find anyone better here." With that she turned, left the kitchen, and locked herself in the bathroom. Charlie left the apartment ten minutes later—Mia heard the front door click shut—but she stayed in there an extra five minutes, just in case he had forgotten something and had to come back. She searched the apartment for her phone, eventually finding it on the floor next to her discarded heels. Mia retreated to the bathroom once more, where she perched on the toilet seat and carefully dialed the numbers written at the top of the receipt she had removed from her jewelry box.

She emerged a few minutes later with the receipt still in her hand, but now scrawled across it in brown eyeliner was: "118B Nguyen Thai Binh, Tan Binh, 9:30." Mia paused as she passed the bedroom. The shirt and tie and trousers she had picked out for Charlie were still arranged on top of the covers, untouched, but his outfit from the night before was missing from the hamper now. Mia walked over to the bed and stretched out alongside the empty clothes. It looked like she was lying next to an invisible man. She snuggled closer and rested her cheek on the breast pocket of the button-up.

"I'm sorry," she breathed. She reached across the shirt to hold its cuff in her hand and listened for a heartbeat beneath the fabric, even though she knew there wouldn't be one.

TWO HOURS LATER, Mia flagged down a taxi and showed the driver the receipt with the address Tuan had given her. The car slipped into the current of morning traffic on Dien Bien Phu, parting the motorbikes like a hand through a swarm of gnats. Mia rested her head against the window and watched the hot sun cooking the various surfaces of the city: tin roofs, asphalt, brown skin.

Outside District 1 there were fewer trees, but tangled power lines hung low across the roads like jungle creepers. The buildings were all skinny and pale yellow, their balconies crowded with strings of drying laundry and red flowers growing in planters made from repurposed water jugs. The taxi's air-conditioning was at full blast; for the first time in ages, Mia felt chilly. She wondered if Tuan would be like Charlie's girls, and expect her to marry him once they had slept together.

Maybe she would, Mia thought to herself, her mind feverish. She would buy a traditional dress and marry Tuan in an incense-choked ceremony. They would rent a one-room apartment in one of these butter-colored buildings. She, too, would hang their laundry out on the balcony and grow red flowers. Her parents would come to see her in Vietnam, her father would give Tuan dirty looks the entire time, and her mother would cry when she saw the rats and the stray dogs and the children running around without pants and the toothless old men holding rooster fights in the street. Mia would have a baby and fill out the paperwork for its American citizenship herself.

The hotel at 118B Nguyen Thai Binh that the taxi pulled up in front of was named—uncreatively—"Hotel." Underneath its sign was another sign, but in Japanese; beneath that was yet another in Korean; and beneath that, Tuan was waiting for her on the sidewalk. He was parked on the same yellow motorbike he had been fixing the day before and which, Mia gathered, was now fully functioning. Mia had never seen him wear a shirt before. A handful of depressed-looking Asian men in suits were milling about in the lobby; the neighborhood they were in seemed to cater to foreign businessmen. Mia liked that she was among outsiders. She began counting out the bills for the driver but paused when, for the first time that morning, she noticed the state of her fingers.

The nails on her right hand were all ragged and ground down. Mia brought them closer to her face; her gold polish was almost all worn away, and her fingertips were rubbed raw. The driver coughed impatiently, so Mia paid quickly and got out of the taxi. She curled her fingers into a fist to hide them.

"My Mia," said Tuan, rising from the motorbike. "I know you will come to me." He held his hand out to her and she took it. Together they entered the cavernous lobby and received a key and a knowing smile from the boy behind the reception desk.

Their fourth-floor room had naked wires sticking out of the wall and heavy dark curtains. A previous guest had left two books behind on the nightstand but the spines were turned away from Mia and she couldn't read the titles. There was no air-conditioning or fan, but for some biological reason Tuan was not sweating the way Mia was. She didn't mind being hot now—it made the decision to take her clothes off easier. While Tuan was locking the door, his back to her, she peeled off her jeans and shirt and left them in a pile on the floor. "You have a condom, right?" she asked.

"I do not know what it is," said Tuan, before turning from the door to her. Immediately, he looked aghast. "Mia! What is wrong with you?!" he cried.

This was not the reaction she had hoped for. Mia looked down at her body. "You don't think I'm beautiful?" she asked, hurt. It was impossible that he didn't. For one insane, brief moment, Mia imagined that Tuan was somehow able to see into her mind, into her heart, and that his horror had been in response to seeing all the ugliness that was there beneath the skin, gnawing a hole somewhere deep and vital inside her.

"What? No! Mia, what is wrong with this?" Tuan was gesturing at the thick layers of gauze Mia had dressed her burn with.

Mia felt embarrassed. "A motorbike." She sat down on the edge of the bed.

Tuan knelt next to her and began unwrapping the bandages on her leg. When he saw the wound he was relieved. "It is not big," he said. "Not bad. Just like a little kiss. But you cannot hide under this, okay?" He waved the gauze pads at her. "If you hide, it will become like mine." He rolled up a sleeve to show her a cluster of small brown scars around his elbow. Mia was skeptical of this medical advice but said nothing. Tuan sat next to her on the bed. "Now," he said with a smile, "what is wrong with *this*?" He brushed the wetness on Mia's cheeks with the back of his hand.

Mia hadn't realized that she was crying. She wiped the tears away; they stung her fingertips. "I have a boyfriend, Tuan."

"It is okay. I have a wife."

"What?!" Mia scooted away from him on the bed, toward the headboard.

"Mia. My Mia. I will explain. Listen to me. I have a wife but we do not have a wedding yet. She lives in my village. My father and mother, and the father and mother of my wife— they are friends. When my wife and I are both little, they make a promise that we will have a wedding someday. Do you understand?"

"An arranged marriage?" Mia was appalled.

He shrugged. "It is business." He shifted on the bed so that he was next to her again.

"What is she like?" asked Mia.

Tuan chewed his lip while he thought. "She is not tall. Her feet are big. She likes cooking. She kills a fish with a knife so quickly. Not the, the . . ." He struggled for a second to remember the word. "Not with sharper part. Like this—" Tuan grabbed Mia's hand and began smacking it with his palm. She presumed that her hand was the fish and that his betrothed spanked it to death with the side of the knife. Tuan was getting excited now; the good part was coming. "Then . . . *WHA!*" He brought the blade of his hand-knife down on her dead hand-fish. "Head is gone! And *ch ch ch ch ch,*" he took the scales off with little flicks of the wrist, even turning it over to make sure both sides were cleaned. His eyes narrowed for a moment when he saw Mia's wrecked nails.

"Tell me more," Mia said, pulling her hand away from him.

"My wife does not know how to swim. She is scared of ghosts. She has hair to . . . here." Tuan placed his hand on Mia's hip to indicate the length and did not remove it when he continued. "She does not speak English but she likes songs from America. When she sings she does not know the words. The drink she likes most is sugarcane juice. When she drives a motorbike it is too fast." He began unbuckling his pants with his free hand. "She is a good daughter. She loves her mother and her father."

"Does she love you?"

"Yes," said Tuan, as he covered Mia's body with his. "And I am sorry."

CHARLIE CALLED THE DAY before Mia left, asking if he could come over to say goodbye and help her pack, which was kind. Mia hadn't expected to see him again. All she'd heard from one of their old mutual acquaintances was that he was living in a little place in District 2 now; when Charlie went away he took all his friends with him. However, he had accidentally left behind Broken-Ear Uncle Ho when he moved out, which Mia thought might partially account for his interest in visiting her.

By the time he got there she had already finished packing; of the five suitcases that Mia had arrived with, only two were leaving Vietnam. She had piled up all the items that weren't coming back with her in the living room like a messy altar— the three discarded suitcases at the bottom, then the laundry basket with most of her clothes; toothpaste and half-empty shampoo bottles and other toiletries that she would replace in America; cups and plates, forks and frying pans; the expensive coffeemaker; and resting serenely atop it all, Uncle Ho's head, wearing the motorbike helmet that Mia hadn't used since Charlie had gone. Her entire collection of high-heeled shoes was littered around the base, all of the soles blackened and scuffed.

Charlie eyed the pile keenly. "Feel free to scavenge," Mia told him. He must have come straight from class; he had his work satchel with him and his necktie was stuffed into his pocket. They sat on the couch and wondered what to say to each other. Mia chewed on a fingernail absently. Charlie had goose bumps on his forearms because the air-conditioning was cranked all the way up.

"You're not bringing back much, huh?" he eventually said, breaking the silence. "Just two bags?"

Mia smiled. "And two carry-ons. But they're very, very small." Just one coin-sized scar on her leg, and one pea-sized embryo in her uterus.

"That's good," Charlie said, rubbing his cold arms.

At the Western clinic the doctor had told her it would look like a little tadpole at this stage, which made Mia think of Tuan's eyes. She had imagined them growing inside her and burst out laughing, and the doctor had given her a funny look. He was a white-haired British man who had come to Vietnam as a specialist in obscure tropical diseases but been forced to switch fields because of the demand in what he called the "field of family planning." Mia found this amusing, too, considering that neither of their plans had worked out as intended. The small pack of white pills he had given her was still unopened; she had wrapped it up in four old receipts and stowed it in her jewelry box, which was now packed inside one of the suitcases.

Charlie studied Mia's face as if he were trying to memorize it. "Will you miss this place at all?" he asked.

Mia did not answer. She stood up and retrieved Broken-Ear Uncle Ho from the pile of abandoned possessions, holding it tenderly in her arms for a moment before laying it on Charlie's lap. "I'll walk with you to your motorbike," she said.

She didn't know which one was the father. In her mind the child would have Tuan's broad nose, his tan skin, his generous lips, and the narrow shape of his eyes, but their color would be the green-blue of Charlie's and its cheeks would bear the faintest trace of freckles. Its soft hair would curl at the ends and possess all of the ten thousand shades between black and brown. Charlie and Mia left her apartment and walked down the stairs side by side. Their hands grazed once. Perhaps neither of them was the father of her child, Mia thought to herself. Perhaps it was the city itself that had spawned it.

While Charlie was tucking Uncle Ho into his satchel, something tumbled out of the bag and fell onto the sidewalk between his motorbike and the wall of the building.

"Let me get it," said Mia, reaching behind the rear wheel. She didn't see the look of panic that crossed Charlie's face. "I think I can . . . Oh!" Her hand had closed around a high heel. When she pulled it out she saw that it was the left shoe of her pair of peach-colored stiletto sandals. There were still indentations worn into the footbed where her toes had once been. "Are you giving these to someone?" Mia asked. "I'm not angry—you can take all of them."

"No! I mean, that's not why I . . . I wasn't . . ." Charlie stammered. He was blushing. "It's not for anyone but me. Look"—he held his satchel open—"I only took one. I slipped it into my bag when you weren't looking so I wouldn't . . . because I still . . ." His voice broke off when he saw that Mia was beaming at him, and then he smiled, too. They stood facing each other on the sidewalk, smiling like fools, glowing in the sunlight, and for one last time they were a couple again and the chaos of the city that surrounded them didn't exist.

"Charlie, I'm—"

But Charlie would never know what she meant to tell him, because a familiar, high-pitched feline wail rose up suddenly from the trash cans on the corner. The cat, which hadn't shown its face in weeks, had returned. Charlie and Mia turned their heads as one of the bins toppled over with a crash and the raggedy tabby crawled out. One of its legs was still gimpy and it looked as if it could barely support its bloated torso. The cat lurched toward them, mewing tremulously and shedding bits of garbage and tufts of its own fur. Mia's fingers tightened around the shoe in her hand.

"You!" As she uttered the word she hurled her sandal at

the creature as hard as she could. It gave a final yowl as the heel clipped its side and then ran into the street, where it was immediately crushed under the wheels of a passing taxi.

Charlie's face was horrified. Mia's was jubilant. Seconds passed. The taxi was long gone—it hadn't even slowed down when it hit the cat.

"Poor thing," said Charlie. Mia reached for his hand but he had already stepped into the street, ignoring the traffic that swarmed around him. She followed even though she didn't need to look.

It wasn't as grisly as she thought it would be. Only the head had been squashed under the tires, and there was barely any blood.

"Goodbye, little cat," said Charlie quietly, bending over the carcass. "I'm so sorry."

But I'm not, thought Mia. *You brought this upon yourself, ugly thing. What did you want from me?*

"God, look how swollen its belly is."

Did you want food?

"Full of parasites, probably."

Did you want to be loved?

"No, not parasites," Charlie said, bringing his face closer. He ran one finger lightly over the curve of the animal's stomach, but it was Mia who shuddered. "I think it—she—was pregnant."

TURNING BACK

———

THOUGH ONE FORTUNATE consequence of my father's disappearance was that we became estranged from his family and whatever nuptials they might incur, given the size of Momma's side there are still at least four weddings to attend each year. Weddings of cousins, weddings of second cousins, weddings of people who are most likely cousins because their last name is Nguyen and they live within a sixty-mile radius. When our family tree was transplanted here from the charred soil of South Vietnam in 1975, it began sprouting with wild abandon; as a result I am now probably related to a third of the greater Houston area by either blood or marriage.

I'm finishing my breakfast and Momma is finishing her dinner when she informs us of another impending union. Cousin Tu is getting married.

"Who's Cousin Tu?" Tommy asks through a mouthful of cereal. I'm not sure which meal this is for him. Possibly lunch.

The last time I saw my older brother was Tuesday morning, and he was eating cereal then, too.

"Cô Ha's oldest son."

"Is he short? Like, *really* short, and kinda fat?"

"I think he goes by 'Dumpling.'"

"Dumpling!" Tommy spews Cheerios. "I know *Dumpling*! I hate that kid!" Momma and I both wait for him to justify his hatred of Dumpling, but Tommy just looks at his watch and then gulps down the rest of his bowl. It's almost half-past nine. I have no positive or negative feelings toward Dumpling. I remember him as one of the older cousins that I rarely spoke to but would see drinking in corners at weddings and funerals and Lunar New Year parties. He is about five feet by three feet in dimension and styles his hair in a poofy crest that does, in fact, resemble the pinched top of a dumpling.

Momma sticks a toothpick in the corner of her mouth and begins to clear the dishes. Later she will wash them in a bucket of water in the bathroom, squatting barefoot on the floor with her hair piled up in a topknot. Old habits from the motherland die hard. When I was in elementary school and still had friends I never invited them over for meals because I was so embarrassed.

"Who's he marrying?" I ask.

Momma begins coiling her hair. It should be mostly gray but she dyes it every week. "Skinny girl. Named Duyen or Quyen or Xuyen," she says through clenched teeth to hold the toothpick in. "The family's from Hue and I can barely understand their Vietnamese. Superstitious bunch, too—they're rushing to have the wedding before one of the great-aunts with liver cancer dies and brings them bad luck."

I wonder if a family death was responsible for Momma's ill-fated marriage to my father. She removes the toothpick to tell us the next part. "So the ceremony's on Saturday morning at eleven. Write it down somewhere before you forget." The toothpick goes back in again. I never actually see Momma clean her teeth with the things—I think she just likes chewing on them.

Tommy gives her one of his patented squinty stares. "Superstitious or not, they couldn't plan a wedding in what, three days? Just how long have you known about it?"

Momma looks guilty. She pretends to be busy with the dishes and says under her breath, "A couple weeks."

"How long?" He's playing patriarch now.

"Maybe a month," she finally admits. Tommy sighs loudly.

Momma looks pouty. "I *meant* to tell you earlier but kept forgetting. I only get to see you and Phuong in the evenings, and I'm tired then." This isn't entirely true; I see Momma most mornings when I get off work. I don't say anything; she only cares if Tommy's there, too.

"Don't you try playing the pity card, kid. It doesn't work on me and Phuong. You raised yourself two cold-blooded killers." What Momma doesn't know is that he's only half joking.

"But you'll be there, right?"

Tommy stands and digs his car keys out of his pocket.

"Right?" Momma wheedles.

"Saturday at eleven," Tommy says and musses Momma's

bun with one hand. When she opens her mouth to complain, the toothpick falls out. Tommy laughs and kisses her on the forehead. He has to bend to reach it. In one smooth movement that he secretly practices, he grabs his jacket from the back of his chair and slings it over his shoulder. I dig my own keys out from under a pile of junk magazines on the table and get stuck in my Texas A&M sweatshirt when I pull it on too quickly. By the time I have my head free and my appendages in the correct sleeves, Tommy's already out the door. I run after him without saying goodbye to Momma.

WHAT YOU SHOULD KNOW about Tommy is that he is the fourth-greatest failure in the family, after Great-Uncle Dong the Communist-Sympathizer, a cousin who went to prison for double homicide, and our own esteemed father. The family's full of gamblers and violent drunkards and deadbeats, but what sets Tommy apart is how much potential he started with, how much he threw away. Back in high school Tommy was Tâm Nguyen Jr., your average piano-playing, calculus-loving, honor-roll–topping, MIT-bound Asian wunderkind. But after graduation, things took a rather unexpected turn. Tommy abruptly shed poor old Tâm Nguyen Jr. like a skin that had grown too tight. He dropped out of MIT after his first semester and moved back home. Stopped speaking Vietnamese and adopted an oily East Texas drawl. Grew his hair long just so he could flip it out of his eyes around the pretty girls. He started disappearing for days at a time, always saying that he'd just been at a cousin's place. Momma still wasn't worried; we have handfuls of cousins—it could have been true. Then he turned up one morning with a stab wound that he blamed on a stapler and told us he was going by "Tommy" now. When the money started coming in, his clothes changed, too. Tâm Nguyen Jr. kept a closet of pressed polo shirts arranged by color, but Tommy prefers things like pinstriped suits. Snakeskin boots. Silk shirts with absurdly high thread counts in the kinds of colors that should get his bony ass jumped in most neighborhoods. Jewelry that even Momma thinks is too flashy. Belts with silver buckles that weigh more than I do.

Underneath his slickster ensembles Tommy is still the skinny Viet nobody he's always been, but he's got everyone fooled now. He has reprobate allure. People don't look at him and see skinny; they see *lithe*. They don't see Vietnamese; they see a borderless brown. Tommy gets along with the Asian kids, with the black kids, with the Mexican kids, with the white kids. It was his talent for getting along with everybody that made him some powerful friends in Houston's shadier circles of not-strictly-legal commerce.

It's no secret that Tommy is now a bottom-of-the-barrel gangster. Everyone in the family knows; even Grandma, who talks to dead people, isn't delusional enough to think that Tommy is an upstanding citizen. Only Momma still believes that he works the night shift at a gas station. For her sake we all just play along. I tell the necessary lies and Tommy pays the rent and Momma can stay happy.

Even his new car hasn't made her the teensiest bit suspicious: a sleek little blue-black convertible that no one on his imaginary salary could afford. He can leave it parked outside because everyone in the neighborhood knows what he does and knows who he knows and wouldn't even think about jacking it. No one ever tries to steal my car, either, but that's because it's a piece of shit and most people would sooner ride a unicycle than be seen driving it. I share Momma's 1987 rust-brown Buick that's shaped like a boat, farts clouds of exhaust, and has a taped-up trash bag in place of a passenger seat window. Tommy christened my car the Drug Deal Mobile and the name stuck. Ironic, considering the activity that his car has seen.

HE'S SITTING SMUG, top down, engine purring, in the driveway as I come out. He hasn't risen quite high enough in the ranks of Assholery to wear sunglasses at night, but he'll be there soon. He laughs while I try to get the door of the Drug Deal Mobile unstuck.

"Picking up chicks in your sweet ride tonight?" he says laughing.

"Shut up!" And then under my breath: "I'm not a lesbian." The door finally opens.

"Then stop dressing like one. I'm gone, kid." With the smoothest of rumbles, Tommy pulls away. It's Thursday night. I probably won't see him again before the wedding on Saturday. I yell at the car for five minutes trying to get it to start. Momma has covered the dashboard with black-and-white pictures of my grandparents on their wedding day and my great-grandmother sitting in a wooden chair, and a crucified Jesus hologram. I yell at them, too, especially toothless wrinkle-bag Great-Grandma, who looks like she's laughing at me. Eventually the car wheezes to life, leaving me fifteen minutes to get to work.

Kwon's World Grocery is off the 610 loop on the Northside. Seven years ago it was Kwon's Kwikmart and the size of a closet, but it swiftly expanded, first taking over the laundromat next door and then the hardware store. Now the only other business left in our little complex is the flashy Fiesta Mart across the parking lot. I often catch Mr. Kwon staring intently at it through the blinds in his office, as if he thinks the building is plotting against him.

Mr. Kwon didn't realize I was a girl until two weeks after I was hired for the night crew. It's understandable: I'm basically boobless and have the same haircut and wardrobe as most thirteen-year-old boys. Plus, the name "Phuong Nguyen" doesn't do much to suggest femininity. You should have seen his expression when I passed in front of him to walk into the women's bathroom.

There are four other fools who work the night shift with me: Akash is the Indian Hulk. At six foot five and roughly three hundred pounds, he has the capacity to destroy the entire grocery store but is generally docile. Instead of getting a ladder on the rare occasions when there's something too high for him to reach, Akash will just toss me up with one arm and I'll grab it.

Jeremy and Sebastian Lee are twins. They don't particularly look alike, but both are convinced that everyone else has them mixed up despite Sebastian's mohawk and the fact that Jeremy is about two inches taller and has violent acne.

And then there's Los, our brooding, Byronic figure on the night shift. Los was Carlos before he left his home in Corpus Christi when he was fifteen, hitchhiked down to Brownsville, and stood at the Mexican border wondering whether to cross, then turned around and started working his way up to Houston. Somewhere along the way he lost half his name. Los is the closest thing I have to a friend, and when I can I drag him along with me to weddings; he goes for the free food and because he knows I can't stand them on my own. Consequently, the faction of my family that doesn't think I'm a lesbian believes Los and I are dating. Both camps are disapproving of my presumed life choices.

Jeremy Lee looks up from unpacking crates of ramen as I walk in. "It's Jeremy, not Sebastian," are the first words out of his mouth.

"I know! God!" I try to slouch past Mr. Kwon's office without him seeing me; he's been living at the grocery store since his wife filed for divorce and only leaves for his court appointments. Too late. He stops glaring at the Fiesta Mart through the window and spots me. I cringe before he even says my name; my efforts to politely correct his pronunciation have been fruitless.

"PWONG!" The way he says it sounds like spit hitting the bottom of a bucket.

"Greetings, Comrade K."

"I have told you before: I don't appreciate your using that term of address. Or that tone."

That's okay; I have plenty more terms of address. "My apologies, Chairman K."

"Very funny, Pwong. Very funny."

I run away to find and bother Los before General Secretary K tries to talk to me about his marital problems. Ever since he discovered I'm a girl he has mistakenly believed that I am sympathetic merely because I own a vagina. It's no wonder I pretend to be a boy.

Los isn't in the sauce aisle. He's not in frozen foods or the aisle devoted to the various incarnations of the soybean. He's by the pineapples with his hood up and his earphones in, so I jump him from behind. He shrugs me off like nothing and I fall onto the linoleum. I bounce up a second later and attack again. This time Los swings me sideways and puts me in a choke hold. "Go play with the Wonder Twins or something—I'm busy."

"We're never busy. What's wrong with you? Estrogen levels out of whack?"

He lets me wiggle free and unplugs his earphones. "Sorry, P. I'm in bad shape tonight. Things have been rough lately." I suppose now's not the time to inform him that he'll be accompanying me to another Nguyen wedding on Saturday.

"Money problems? Syphilis? Existential angst?"

For a minute he mulls over whether he should tell me or not. "Girl problems," he finally admits.

"Ha! Knew you were PMSing!"

Los pulls the hood of my sweatshirt up and yanks hard on the drawstrings so I can't see. "You don't know anything about it," he says, and kicks me in the direction of the vegetables.

I run off to attend to the very important business of putting things onto shelves. Restocking is boring, but I'm too scrawny to unload the trucks. Akash and Los are responsible for that, and JerBastian and I move things from the storeroom to the shelves. It sounds simple enough, but things always go to pieces before the dawn—literally, in the case of Akash, who accidentally destroys a crate of something at least once a night. The Lees bicker constantly and drag race in shopping carts when Commissar K is preoccupied. Los is fine unless he's in a mood, like tonight, and then he starts sneaking sips from a flask. By four we're all sick of one another and cursing in our respective mother tongues until four thirty, when the seafood trucks come and we put aside our differences to unpack the crates of salmon and shrimp and things with tentacles. At six we'll emerge blinking in the early sunlight, nod to the denizens of the Fiesta Mart night shift in the parking lot, and then scuttle off to whichever highway exit we call home.

When Momma asks I tell her that the job's only temporary, that of course I want to go back to school soon—that's why I still wear my sweatshirt—but it's always a lie. I was a part of that daylight world for a long time. It's full of things like slow traffic and hot sun on office buildings and kids going to swim practice and divorce settlements and weddings. I have no interest in any of that. I choose the comfortable little universe of Kwon's instead, where nothing ever changes except for the seasonal produce.

TONIGHT THE HOURS GLIDE BY. At midnight I get hungry and steal an apple and a packet of weird-tasting chips from the Korean snack food aisle. At two Los stops drinking after he knocks over half a dozen bottles of fish sauce and says that Akash did it. At three thirty I call Sebastian "Jeremy" on purpose and he refuses to talk to me until the shrimp truck arrives. At five he and Jeremy take over the PA system and pump reggaeton until Benevolent Dictator K wakes up from a nap and puts an end to it.

And then at five thirty I take out the garbage and there is an old Asian man, completely naked, crouched by the dumpster.

We both look at each other for a moment in frozen panic. Then I let out a gargly half scream and everything starts moving again. I'm looking for something to hit him with and I can't stop yelling and my legs are doing a jittery grapevine and I'm digging around in the garbage bag because I know there's an old daikon radish in there and I'm going to throw it.

"Please! Please! Miss! Oh please don't!" the naked man begs.

I realize two things: That he has recognized me as a girl.

And that he's speaking in Vietnamese. I stop yelling but I don't release the daikon, which I'm clenching like a grenade. The man slowly stands, keeping himself covered with both hands. He looks about seventy, with close-cropped white hair and wrinkled skin loosely concealing the pointy suggestions of bones. I've never seen this much saggy grandpa-meat before and never want to again.

"What the fuck are you doing here?" I squeak out in English, because I am far too freaked out to manage Vietnamese.

"I apologize for startling you," he says, switching into careful English, too. "I realize that I may not be able to convince you of my sanity, but rest assured, I mean you no harm. Now, if it's not too much trouble, could you help me find some clothes?" He doesn't sound like a serial rapist.

"Are you homeless?"

"No, no, not exactly."

"What are you doing here, and why are you naked?"

He smiles politely, vaguely, as if I've just asked him about the weather or his weekend plans. "I have a condition," he says.

"Sleepwalking?"

"It's slightly more complicated."

"Yeah? You get your sick kicks perving around dumpsters in the middle of the night?"

The naked stranger seems taken aback. The settings dial in my brain has been stuck in the Aggression/Insolence position for so long, sometimes I forget how I come across to other people.

"My child," he says, "I promise you, this isn't a . . ." He struggles for words for a moment. "It's nothing as predictable as that. This affliction that I suffer from has a story behind it, and not a pleasant one. It's not of a sexual nature, but it still isn't the sort of thing that nice young girls like to hear."

I flutter my eyelashes faux-coquettishly. "Do I strike you as particularly nice or girly?"

"My child, I'm just trying to clothe myself before the sun comes up." There is a note of panic in his voice.

I take my sweatshirt off and toss it to him. I'm only doing this because in the back of my mind I feel the twinge of the old Motherland Complex: Respect your elders. I'd thought I'd kicked the habit, but I guess not.

He can't catch the sweatshirt because his hands are clasped over his crotch, so it lands with a soft whump on the ground in front of him. For some reason this feels almost more embarrassing than finding him here naked in the first place. "I'm going to go find you pants," I say. "Against my better judgment."

"I am, of course, much obliged."

As I turn to go back into the store I take a moment to hurl the daikon with all my strength at the wall, where it smashes and leaves a satisfying white smear on the brick. I hope he flinched. Once inside I head for aisle 16, grabbing a bottle of grape soda along the way.

Beneath the large sign that says "Appliances" is another, smaller one reading: "and Bidet World." This refers to the display of high-tech Japanese toilets for sale but sounds more like the world's most disturbing amusement park. After a quick look around to make sure I'm alone, I pour the contents of the soda bottle into the tanks of the two demo models and remove the plastic shields from the bowls. Then I press down hard on both control panels, mashing all of the buttons at once, and run away as the toilets erupt into fountains of purple.

I burst into Premier K's office, breathless. "One of the Lees was fooling around in Bidet World again. I can't get the toilets to turn off." They always get the credit for my best ideas.

"What?!" The Japanese toilets are his pride and joy. Fearless Leader K charges out the door in a fury to find and throttle whichever twin he locates first, and I take the opportunity to steal a pair of his pants. He is living out of three suitcases and some boxes stacked in the corner, and while I suppose most people would find this sort of sad, it makes my task much easier. I grab a pair of khakis that look like they won't be missed and shimmy out of the office. Naked Dumpster Grandpa is just going to have to live without underwear—unusual as the situation may be, there are still some lines I refuse to cross.

I'm feeling fairly pleased with myself until I return to the back lot and discover that he has disappeared. For a moment I am furious, thinking that he's run off without telling me his story, leaving me with two exploding bidets and Generalissimo K's pants, but then he pokes his upper half—now sporting my sweatshirt—out from where he had been concealing himself. I am relieved, which should never be your reaction to seeing a half-nude septuagenarian. I come closer and throw him the balled-up khakis. He catches them, vanishes behind the dumpster, and reemerges fully clothed a minute later. I notice that he is also wearing a pair of grimy plastic slippers and wrinkle my nose. "I assume those came out of the trash?"

He nods. "I took the liberty of rummaging while you were gone."

Sunrise is arriving early, in streaks, and both my shift and my duty to this old man are over. I'm smart enough to know that this is where I should abandon the shenanigans and go home to Momma before I get mixed up in something I'll regret. But I feel intoxicated by the weirdness of the past hour. I'm not ready for it to stop just yet. "So, Mister . . ."

"Hiep. Vo Van Hiep. Originally from Bac Lieu province."

"I'm Phuong. So, Ông Hiep from the Bac Lieu province, are you going to explain your 'condition' to me here, or over dinner?"

"Dinner?"

"Breakfast technically. But it's dinner for me. There's a place right down the road owned by some of my second cousins with good *bún bò*. Let's go."

He raises an eyebrow. "You're the first person I've encountered who can make an invitation sound like a threat. And do you think it's really wise to invite out someone you've only just met, and under such circumstances?"

The answer is fairly obvious but I'm not about to admit it. "My car's out front. It's the brown Buick that smells as bad as your garbage slippers. Wait for me there while I grab my stuff inside."

—

I WAS WRONG: THE shoes smell much worse than the Drug Deal Mobile. Thankfully, the restaurant is only five minutes away, but I drive with my head out the window anyway.

The place is dim and smells like pork fat and dishwater. The walls are covered with old, greasy-looking photographs of familiar Vietnamese landmarks: Ha Long Bay, One-Pillar Pagoda, the post office in Saigon, the floating market. We are the only customers and take a table by the window. It's been so long since I've been like this—excited, nervous, quivery, nauseous in a way that doesn't stop me from eating—that it takes me a while to remember the name of the feeling: anticipation. I have to force myself to wait until Ông Hiep has finished half of his bowl of soup before probing. "Tell me."

Ông Hiep takes his time. He calls over the waiter and orders tea and I wait in squirmy silence until it comes. He props his elbows up on the table, holds the mug with both hands, and then leans forward to lightly rest his chin on the rim. "I could tell you the truth. You wouldn't believe it and you would dismiss me as a lunatic and it would most certainly ruin the meal." He pauses and raises one tufty white eyebrow. "It doesn't have to be that way. We could just sit here and finish our soup, making pleasant and meaningless conversation. Afterward, you would kindly take care of the check—as I have no means of paying you—and allow me to keep these clothes. And then we would part: you, entertained by the events of this morning, I, forever grateful for your generosity, and neither of us the worse for it. It's up to you." He puts his mug down. "However, I fear that you are the curious type."

I lay my chopsticks across the top of my bowl, fold my hands, and give him a double-barreled-shotgun stare. Tommy isn't the only one who can play Yakuza. "I want to know everything."

His eyes disappear into his wrinkles when he smiles. "I see. But you must remember, later, that it was you who insisted on knowing." He looks out the window for a long moment. When he turns back to me his smile is gone. "*Ach,* there is no delicate way to say it. The condition that I suffer from is this: Periodically, I will transform from a man into a snake. It is something that has happened to me since my youth in Vietnam. The episodes are irregular, but on average I make the change a couple of times every month. From a handful of occasions when I awoke human again, but tangled up in a molted snakeskin, I know for certain that I take the form of a reticulated python of about fourteen feet in length—rather on the small side, considering that the adult species can grow to over twenty feet. Do you have questions or shall I just continue? Or perhaps having heard only this much you wish to leave?"

I hold his gaze, waiting for him to crack, to laugh uproariously at his own crazy joke. But he doesn't. His face is tired and lined and dead serious. I shake my head no. Go on.

"It always happens like this: Sometime in the night I will suddenly be overcome with spasms, unable to make a sound. My body will twist and my bones contort, my arms cleave to my sides and my legs to each other, and my skin grows tight, and I watch helplessly as it hardens into a thousand scales. There is a terrible pulling. Then the change is complete and I am aware of nothing until I regain consciousness as a man once more, without my clothes and often in an unfamiliar place. The last time, I was discovered in the branches of an oak tree down in the Third Ward. I usually transform back into a man within ten hours, but sometimes I am the python for days before I come to. Which reminds me—what is today's date?"

I locate my voice, way back in my throat. "The twelfth. Thursday."

He reaches for his tea and drinks deeply. When he speaks again I can tell that he is trying very hard to keep his voice steady. "And the month?"

"April."

He says nothing but returns to staring out the window. The rest of Houston is up now, and when trucks hurtle past on the highway the glass rattles.

"Can you remember what it's like?" I ask. "Afterward?"

Ông Hiep doesn't move, but slowly a smile begins to spread over his face, a slow, helpless smile that exposes him more than any physical nakedness ever could. "Bits. They come back to me like pieces of a dream. You couldn't really call them memories. Just ghosts of sensations that the human body cannot know. How to taste smell, how to taste heat. Seeing the world in motion, not in colors, not in shapes. To move like a ripple over the earth. The feeling of coiling, of lengthening, of squeezing." His smile fades.

"The first transformation was when I was eighteen. I woke up just before dawn in my father's banana grove, about a mile and a quarter from our house, naked and in excruciating pain. For a while I lay there, trying to remember if I had been drinking. And then it came back to me: The cramps that had wrenched me awake in the night. Voiceless screaming. Writhing. Falling from my bed to the floor, praying that the noise would wake someone. Nobody coming. Feeling my clothes come loose and slip off as my body elongated and my bones rearranged themselves. Swallowing in fear, and realizing with horror that the saliva did not stop at my throat, for I no longer had one. Alone beneath the banana trees, I remembered, and I wept. At the pain, yes, and the confusion and terror of it all. But also because even though I was set in my old flesh again, somewhere very deep inside me, something was different. I don't know if it was something gained or lost or awakened, but it was changed regardless. At sunrise I stole home, put on my old clothes, and lay in bed as I waited for the rest of the house to rise. After that first episode I began praying feverishly for hours each day.

"You should know that my family was part of the small Catholic minority in Bac Lieu. My eldest brother was a priest. We all could recite the beginning of the book of Genesis by heart. I knew what the Bible said about the serpent: that for its cunning, God condemned it to crawl for all eternity. I didn't know why He had cursed me with this form which He so despised, what sin I had committed to deserve such a punishment. I fasted and burned incense to my ancestors, prostrating myself before their tombs and begging for forgiveness. But two weeks later I changed again.

"This time it did not go completely unnoticed. One of my brothers discovered thick, S-shaped tracks in the mud at the edge of one of our fields. The village was frightened; snakes of that size were rare in our part of the East, and though it was unlikely that one alone could kill a strong man, it would go after chickens, goats, dogs, even children. Three weeks passed. Four weeks. Five. I allowed myself to believe that the other nights had been nothing but vivid hallucinations. But the next time I transformed, I woke up at the edge of the forest and I was not alone: My arms and legs were wrapped tightly around the corpse of a girl. I knew her, too—she was the younger sister of a friend. She was covered in bruises; every single bone in her body had been crushed. As I cradled the poor broken girl, sobbing, I slowly became aware of a strange ache around my mouth and lower jaw, a soreness that I hadn't felt after the other transformations. And then I realized what it meant and I threw back my head and screamed. I had been trying to eat her.

"I fled into the forest and never returned to my village. I spent the next years wandering, begging, stealing. Trying and failing to take my own life. But I couldn't go on despising myself forever. Eventually I stopped asking God for forgiveness.

"Do you know that the first people of Vietnam worshipped the snake? You see, we aren't so dissimilar, God and I—both feared and revered. But what I came to realize—what He never knew—is that freedom is this slippery form he gave me. His punishment was really His greatest gift. The warm-blooded life is nothing precious by comparison—it is made easily, brutally. He creates by ripping, splitting, by tearing life away from its mother's belly, by dividing and then giving breath. And I am precisely the opposite, taking life away by clutching at it too tightly, returning it to the belly and making us one again, embracing it until the breath is gone." He has been gradually tightening his grip on his mug of tea and the veins on the back of his hand bulge beneath the skin. A wild, desperate gleam appears in his eyes. "Do you believe me, Phuong?"

His question catches me by surprise and I don't get a chance to lie. "Yes."

"If you believe what I am, then you must be afraid."

I probably should be. But when I pause and evaluate I decide that although I'm not sure exactly what I'm feeling yet, I know it isn't fear. "No."

"Are you repulsed by me?"

"No."

"Not fear, not revulsion. Do you pity me then?"

I look at his tiny white head poking out from the immense maroon cowl of my sweatshirt. I wonder if he's been hurt before, here, in this city. Most of my family would shoot a snake on sight if it was too big to beat to death with a shovel. "No," I say again.

Ông Hiep releases his breath and the crazy goes out of his eyes. Other people have entered the restaurant. I'm sure most of them assume that I'm a good grandkid, probably with a high GPA, taking Pop-Pop out for breakfast. They'll never know the real story, and this exhilarates me. I try to name this feeling, this buzzing in my blood as I sit in a nameless Vietnamese soup restaurant in north Houston, and then I realize that's just it—it's feeling. It's not something I'm used to and it scares me more than anything Ông Hiep has told me.

I try to ignore it. "How did you end up in Texas?" I ask. "But maybe tell me the abbreviated version—I have to get home soon because my mother uses the car during the day."

"It was back in the late fifties. Smugglers caught me in python form; I woke up in a crate in the cargo hold of a ship, about two hours away from being turned into a handbag. They let me out in Galveston and even gave me fake paperwork, they were so scared." He laughs, remembering. "Superstition can be a useful thing." He takes one last sip of tea, draining the mug. "I'm being rude," he says. "I've hogged the entire conversation. Why don't you tell me some of your secrets?"

"I don't have any secrets. And I don't have any were-snake powers."

He laughs. "How old are you?"

"Nineteen."

"It could still happen. You work at the grocery store overnight?"

"It's a job."

"Unusual, isn't it?"

"Why? Because I'm a 'nice young girl'?"

"Doesn't your family mind?"

"Why are we playing Inquisitor General all of a sudden?"

"I guess I'm the curious type, too. And, well, I've already laid myself bare . . ."

I grimace. "I don't need to be reminded."

Ông Hiep chuckles to himself before giving me an inscrutable look. "You see, I am just a very old man who is sometimes a python. But you, my child, are a creature far more complex."

"Ha!" I exclaim. "Prepare to be underwhelmed. My family doesn't care if I'm out all night stocking shelves; it's a respectable occupation, considering what most of them do. I have one older brother. He's a small-time crook, does things like fetching the coffee and the dry-cleaning and cocaine for the mob bosses, but he dresses as if he knows the Godfather personally. My mother runs a nail salon, feeds us, and the rest of the time behaves like an overgrown child. I'm up to my ears in cousins who insist on getting married all the time, so I spend half my life suffering through their various weddings and engagement ceremonies. You probably know some of the extended family. Or you might have a third cousin or something who married one of mine."

"That would be unlikely—to my knowledge none of my family made it out of Vietnam, and I never married or had children. Although . . ." He looks cagey.

"What?"

"There's no shortage of female pythons in the jungles of Vietnam. Perhaps in my snake form I was, well, luckier."

I grimace again.

"It's just nature," he says. "I notice that you didn't mention your father. Was that on purpose?"

"It's because he's absent."

"I'm sorry. Is it painful or is it something you can talk about?"

"Not painful, no. It's the opposite of that. All right, I'll tell you about Old Papa Tâm, but first, I need to know something: Have you ever thought about going back? To Vietnam?"

Ông Hiep looks pensive for a moment. "Thought about it, yes, but deep down I've always known that when I left I left for good."

"Why?"

"Well, even if the war had ended differently I probably wouldn't have returned, but after 1975 there was no question about it. It isn't my home anymore. I am almost certain that my old village was destroyed, that many of the people I loved died in ways I do not wish to dwell upon. If there are any who remain, they think I have been dead for over fifty years. I would be lost in that place. What happened in Vietnam was unthinkable, Phuong. Inhuman. Something that terrible and strange changes everything in a way that makes going back impossible."

"That's just it!"

"It is?"

"It is. Here's the thing: It would have been one thing if Tâm Nguyen Sr. had just walked out on us. Left my momma for another woman. Abandoned us and moved to, I don't know, Tucson. Los Angeles. Buffalo. That, I would be able to understand. But when he left us it was to go back. He left us for Vietnam. I didn't—I still don't—quite believe it. My father grew up in a country that was on fire. He helped find the limbs of a cousin who made the mistake of playing with an unexploded shell. He sacrificed everything he had to get out. He pushed his younger brother out of the way to make it onto the boat. I remember how he used to lock himself in his room on the Fourth of July because the sound of the fireworks reminded him too much of bombs. Vietnam was his nightmare. It's easier for me to believe that you sometimes turn into a giant snake than to believe that he could want to go back."

My eyes are starting to prickle dangerously. I suspected this might happen, but it's too late to stop now. "He said he was going to Saigon to start a business. Everyone tried to talk him out of it. His job here paid well; he had two kids to look after and a wife who didn't know how to use a dishwasher. They told him he was plain crazy for returning to that dark place voluntarily. No one could convince him.

"For a while we got regular, crackly phone calls and a check every month. He told us that the work—catfish exporting, or something like that—was still getting off the ground but doing well. That he would come home soon and visit. He said he had presents for me. And then after six months it all stopped. The phone calls, the money, everything. I'm sure that Momma tried. She never heard back from his business partners, never got anything useful out of the American Consulate. She dug up all her old contacts who were still living in Saigon, but none of them could tell us anything. Maybe she should have flown over there herself and started looking under stones and poking around the riverbeds. It would have been about as effective. It's easier than you think to vanish completely in America; imagine how easy it is to disappear in a place like Vietnam. He knew that when he left, and he still went." I wipe my nose. "It isn't painful for me, I told you that already. I just don't understand it. Let's get the check now. I think I'm done with secrets."

WE BUY TIME IN the parking lot outside the restaurant. He shuffles his feet and I jangle my keys, and in a creepy way it reminds me of that awkward moment at the end of a first date when you don't know whether to kiss or hug or shake hands and leave quickly. Not that I've been on a lot of dates—most guys aren't too keen on taking out girls who look like their younger brothers.

I can't leave him, now that we know what we do about each other.

"Do you need a ride home?" I ask Ông Hiep.

"I feel like I've already pushed your generosity far enough, and didn't you say that you need to get the car to your mother?"

I remember the conversation from breakfast last night. If Momma can forget that she sees her daughter every morning, then her daughter can easily forget to come home. I take my cellphone out of my pocket and turn it off. "No," I say.

He gives me a long look. "Thank you," he finally says, and reaches for the car door.

"Wait—lose those nasty shoes before you get in." Then I have a better idea. "On second thought, give them to me."

We get on the freeway and I weave around the lanes until I'm in front of somebody's big shiny Ford pickup. I haven't played highway basketball in a while but I'm pretty sure I'll make the shot—it's not too windy and the slippers are the perfect weight. Tommy and I used to do this all the time, back in his early days of physics nerd-dom. He was so strategic about it, so sure that his theories of aerodynamics and trajectory algorithms and whatnot meant that he couldn't lose, but he always did anyway. I hold the slippers out the window with my left hand, as high as I can. From the dashboard, my grandparents, great-grandma, and hologram Jesus watch me disapprovingly.

"It's not going to work!" says Ông Hiep. He has to yell over the sound of the wind beating against the garbage-bag–covered window.

"You just watch!" I release the shoes and the wind takes them. One flies crooked and I see it tumbling around over near the railing. But the other goes straight back and skims the top of the Ford as it comes roaring up behind us. I switch lanes and slow down. "Check it! Check it! Is it on the ground?"

Ông Hiep swivels in his seat to look out the back window. "I don't see the other shoe anywhere," he admits.

"Louder!"

"I don't see it!"

"Yes! I got it in the truck bed! Told you I could!"

He chuckles at first but lets his laughter fade into something like long, broken sighs. "This is what your life is, isn't it? Games. You're just playing."

"I can't hear you!"

"Playing! All you do is play!"

"Yes," I say softly, not bothering to yell because I know he can read it on my lips.

AT ÔNG HIEP'S INSTRUCTION I get off 610 somewhere around the northeast side and then spend forty minutes lost in the Fifth Ward while he tries to remember the directions to his house. We pass through neighborhoods where gentrification has been poking its nose around, and neighborhoods that still look like the ancestral homeland of the Drug Deal Mobile. Eventually we find a road he knows and follow it to a scabby collection of boxy one-story houses by the train tracks. Ông Hiep points to one that looks like it used to be painted blue. "There."

I lock the car, even though the street is mostly deserted. Only a mother and her chubby toddler sit on their porch next door and watch us. "Ah, good," Ông Hiep says quietly. "I worry each time that I've eaten Mrs. Alvarez's baby. Good morning, Ana!" he calls out, and Mrs. Alvarez nods. He turns back to me. "I suppose, then, that this is where we part ways."

No, no, no, not yet. "Let me wash my hands inside first. I can't believe I touched those shoes without gloves. I probably have hep C." I push past him and scamper up the porch steps. "Hey, your door's unlocked . . ."

No one has been here in a very long time. There are cobwebs in the corners, and it's dark and smells like microbes. I cross the room and open a window to let some air in. "Ông Hiep, when was the last—when did you—"

"Forty-five days," he says from the doorway. "The longest it's been yet. I'm afraid that, honest though I've been, there is something I haven't told you, Phuong." He steps inside and walks over to sit on the only furniture in the room, a high, old-fashioned sofa, leaving prints in the dust with his bare feet. I come and sit down next to him. He places his hand over mine and I realize it's the first time we've touched. His skin is cool and dry and surprisingly smooth.

"For the past several years I have been making the change far more frequently, and remaining in my snake form for increasingly prolonged stretches of time. I have come to accept—in fact, I always suspected it—that someday, someday very soon, I am going to transform one final time. And when I do I will not be turning back. Wait, don't say anything yet."

I am yawning, not trying to speak, but I don't correct him.

"I will certainly be captured or killed sooner or later." He pauses and then suddenly bursts out laughing. "I didn't mean for that to sound quite so martyrly," he says when he has collected himself. "It's just a fact. They will catch me. It's already remarkable—and more than a little disconcerting—that I have survived for so long. I am either a very clever python or this is a very unobservant city."

Careful not to move my hand from under his, I wiggle to a more comfortable position on the sofa. Ông Hiep doesn't seem to notice. He continues: "If I'm lucky, I will be discovered and Animal Control will be called in before I kill or injure somebody, and I will be able to live out the rest of my reptilian years in a zoo somewhere. Or perhaps I will promptly meet my end beneath the tires of some behemoth truck."

I have adjusted myself so that my head is on the armrest now, and I don't see any harm in closing my eyes for a moment. "I'm still listening," I murmur. I feel the cushions shift as Ông Hiep stands up.

He tucks my arm at my side and releases my hand. "I'm glad I had the chance to meet you, Phuong," he says. "I wish that it had happened earlier, and under different circumstances. But I hope that today will be the last time we cross paths. I don't want to consider the possibility of what would happen should you encounter me in my other form. You are quite small."

"I'm going to miss you, Ông Hiep," I say, only semi-aware of the words that leave my mouth. "And I don't ever miss people."

"Perhaps it's time you started to, Phuong. I know it's frightening, but perhaps it's time you changed."

"Ông Hiep, would I make a good python?" I ask through another yawn.

"Hmm. I think you would be a different sort of snake. Something small. Something fast. Something poisonous. Something good at disguising itself."

Sleep is coming quickly now, laying itself heavy on my bones, dulling my brain, but my voice continues on without its consent: "I'll never be able to talk about what happened today. Not with anyone. Because they wouldn't believe it." It feels like I'm telling myself my own bedtime story. "They would think it was something twisted. Something bad. Even though there's nothing wrong with us. Nothing wrong at all. But they'd think it was just because I'm a girl, even if I don't look like one. And just because you're an old man."

"It's funny," he says, and it's the last thing I hear before I fall asleep, "but sometimes I wonder if I am actually a man, or if I'm a snake who is just pretending all the other times."

A CHILLY BREEZE THROUGH the open window wakes me hours later. My mouth tastes crusty and disgusting and my lips are all dry. I blink slowly, adjusting my eyes to the darkness. Darkness? I pat my pockets to find my phone and turn it on. Quarter to eight already. "Ông Hiep?" I call softly first, then louder when I hear no answer. I hold up my phone, shining the weak, bluish light from the screen around the room: emptiness and dust and there, in the corner, a large, dark mass that wasn't there earlier. I bite my lip and extend my arm with the phone a little farther. As my eyes make sense of the shadows, the large mass reveals itself to be folds of fabric—my Texas A&M sweatshirt and Mr. Kwon's khakis, in a heap on the ground.

I swallow, hard, and then sit as still as I can, listening. Where are you? I can barely hear over the sound of my own heartbeat. Where are you hiding? There's nothing in the room except the sofa.

Oh God, the sofa. I quickly yank my legs up off the ground

and curl into a ball against the armrest, holding myself as tightly as I can. When my pulse has calmed down I lean as far out from the sofa as I dare, trying to see beneath it. There are about eight inches between the frame and the floor. Plenty of space. I can't see anything scaly in the blackness but I don't know if that's a good thing or a bad thing. What I do know is that I'd prefer not to stick my head underneath to find out. I return to the fetal position and squeeze my cellphone. Who would I call? The police? Momma? I'm not even sure exactly where I am.

I'm all out of tricks. Rigging toilets and throwing shoes can't help me now. And it was my own decision, by the dumpster, that brought me down this path and deposited me here, in a dark house with a creature that doesn't need to see to find me. I remember now how back at the restaurant he offered me the choice to walk away. To not know. But there was no choice, really. I wanted this. I was looking for this place, this knowledge, this feeling, the whole time.

I'm going to have to run for it, and the desperation thrills me. Still, I cannot rush. In measured, torturously slow movements, I stand up on the sofa, ready for a giant primeval reptile to erupt out from underneath it at any second. When nothing happens I can finally exhale. I balance with my toes on the edge of the seat cushion. The elaborate plan I've devised is to leap as far as I can off the sofa and then sprint the rest of the way. I crouch, ready to jump. Then I panic and straighten my legs again; it has suddenly occurred to me that the dust on the ground could make me slip and fall, leaving me easy prey. I brandish my phone again, shining the light on the floorboards to gauge the danger. And that's when I see the marks.

I don't know how I missed them the first time—even in the pathetic glow of the phone they are visible: huge, clumsy S-shapes rubbed away in the film on the floor. I aim the light around the base of the sofa again; the only prints in the dust there were left by feet. He isn't under me after all. I turn the phone toward the door again and study the tracks from my vantage point on the sofa. They start in the area surrounding the clothes as a mess of indistinct squiggles and gradually become one clean, sine-wave–shaped track. I follow the sinuous line with my eyes a little farther: They lead directly to the open window. Oh, well done, you.

I need to bury my face in my hands and shudder with both relief and fresh terror for a moment, but after that I'm ready. Running seems unwise, now that I don't know where I should be running away from. I put one foot on the floor, and then the other, and begin to take cautious steps, pausing between each one to listen for rustling in the darkness. My phone I keep held out in front of me, like an evil-repelling amulet. When I finally put my hand on the doorknob I half-expect the creature to lash out from where it was hiding, watching me the entire time and allowing me to think I would escape. But the knob turns easily and I step outside into the smoggy Houston twilight. Because I grew up here I know not to bother gazing at the night sky, but my father never lost the habit of looking up and expecting to see stars.

I almost let myself breathe easy. I almost lose control, dash for the car, jump in, and floor it. Luckily I restrain myself because there is something suspicious about the Drug Deal Mobile. More suspicious than usual, that is. I come a little closer to confirm it—my trash-bag window has been almost completely pushed in. It hangs from the last bits of remaining tape like a super ghetto cat flap. I found you.

As I approach the car I am stealthy, cool. I circle up toward the driver's side. All I want is a quick peek, a glimpse, a coil, a scale, a flickering of the tongue. I need to know for certain that he's in there. But before I can, something—something heavy-sounding inside the Drug Deal Mobile—goes thump and I sprint away before I realize what I'm doing.

I flee down the poorly lit street lined with dilapidated houses. I run and run, and my sneakers pound the asphalt so hard that one comes loose and falls off, and then the other. I keep running. I don't even look down. My feet hurt at first, but after a while I can't feel them anymore. It occurs to me that I might be transforming. I stop and examine my body, panting. No, I am still two legs, two arms, with sweat in my hair and running down into my eyes. I wipe it away roughly with a sleeve.

"Phuong!"

For a moment I think it's him. For a moment I believe that when I turn around he'll be there, and he'll be himself again. But it's not him. It's Tommy.

"Phuong! Fuck!" He grabs me by the shoulders. "What the hell are you doing here? Shit shit shit. Shit! Fuck!" He sounds like he's malfunctioning. "You cannot be here. You just—it's not—fuck!—this is not a good place for you, okay? Okay?" He is steering me toward the corner where his fancy little car is parked. "How did you get here? Hey!" Tommy grabs me by the biceps. "Where's your car?" He shakes me. I shake my head.

Tommy opens the door and shoves me inside. He studies my face. "Are you hurt?" I shake my head again and he checks to make sure that all my parts have made it in the car before shutting the door. He walks around and climbs behind the steering wheel.

"Don't take me home!" I blurt out suddenly. Tommy gives me a look. He uses both hands to comb his hair back and then starts the engine.

"I was working just now," he says as he navigates the dark streets with an ease that betrays how well he knows this part of the city. "And we saw this little delinquent-looking kid come running like hell down the street." He is staring hard through the windshield at nothing in particular now. "They told me to go take care of it and sent me outside. Do you get it, Phuong? Do you get what that means? Do you get what could have happened?" He takes his hand off the wheel and purposefully brushes the bottom of his jacket back just enough for me to see the grip of the handgun. When he is satisfied that I understand, he continues: "This is the kind of place when, at a certain time of night, if you're where you shouldn't be, you disappear." We're getting back on the 610 loop now. "Can you tell me what you were doing there?"

I look at my lap and shake my head.

"Okay," Tommy says. "I get it. I have my secrets, you have yours. But you're going to have to promise me that you won't go back."

"I won't."

"That's good enough for me. So if we aren't going home, where should we go?"

"Can we just drive? Around?"

"At least until one of us gets a better idea."

The night is really beginning now. The nine-to-fivers are back at home already; the only ones out at this time are the ones who have run away from that life. Somewhere in Houston neon lights are going on. Mr. Kwon stands in his grocery store kingdom and looks out the window. Momma is falling asleep alone. My fat cousin Dumpling's bride lays out her wedding dress for tomorrow. Her great-aunt with liver cancer continues breathing. Something that used to be a man twines in the seat of an old, abandoned car. Some gangsters wonder where one of their own has gone off to. My older brother and I drive.

We drive around the warehouses by the water. We drive through the dark parts of the city and watch couples stumbling out of nightclubs in each other's arms and prostitutes slinking in the shadows, looking for arms that need someone to hold. We drive too fast down deserted expanses of the freeway and I let my right arm hang out of the window, cupping the night and the wind in my fingers while lights that are not stars twinkle all around me. Usually I would be able to pretend it's beautiful. But tonight it's not enough to distract me anymore. As we circle endlessly on 610, all I can think of is how much the highway resembles a snake coiling around the entire city.

ONE-FINGER

———

THE VERY SMALL CITY lay tucked among the green-gray folds of the central highlands. At night, were one to observe it from above and from a distance, the gently pulsing lights of the town would resemble a luminescent mold spreading over the hills. The people who inhabited this particular region of the country, high above the steamy reach of the Mekong but still far from the bitter northern winter, were tempered by their climate. They shared most of their lives with a perpetual, damp chill—the kind of bleak and persistent cold that never quite reaches the bone but instead lodges somewhere just beneath the skin from September through April.

But this particular December night was colder than it should have been. Breath turned pale before it left the mouth and lingered on in a white cloud even after its maker had walked away. The streets were mostly deserted, and those still outside hurried home quickly, eager to escape from the biting wind. It was so unnaturally chilly that the Guitarist, perched on a wooden stool in the Calligrapher's living room, was wearing a wool glove over his strumming hand, which slowed his already clumsy playing considerably. The Poet had arrived early and claimed the couch—he reclined, keeping both hands warm in the pockets of his tweed jacket and feeling lucky that his particular role did not require him to remove them. Perhaps the Calligrapher did not feel the cold, for he sat on the tile floor facing his two friends, his legs folded underneath the low table before him. Shriveled and arthritic though he was, the Calligrapher was never still. Even at rest he was possessed by a manic, rodentlike energy, always twitching something, drumming his fingers, gnawing on the inside of his cheek. Even in his sleep his hands would play with the keys he wore on a long chain around his neck. He was jiggling his knee now, knocking it against the tabletop from below. The objects crowding the table's surface—a pot of ink, a bottle of crude Vietnamese vodka, half empty, a single shot glass, and a stack of white paper—trembled with each movement.

The canny observer might detect that brushes were absent from the table, but also that the Calligrapher's left hand was stained black to varying degrees—the index finger dyed past its bony knuckle, the pad of the thumb colored a darkness that would never wash away, and the outer side of the palm marked with coin-sized splotches. The discoloration of the hand gave the impression that it was in the process of rotting.

Once, the Poet had been the handsomest of the three, but now his bloated body strained against the seams of his jacket and his belly was almost indistinguishable from the couch cushions. The Guitarist was neither as shriveled as the Calligrapher nor swollen like the Poet. He had a drooping mustache and a mole on his chin from which several long white hairs sprouted.

There was no place for forced cordiality in the Calligrapher's living room. The three knew one another far too well; they had been meeting like this for too many years. The Guitarist and the Poet did not bother knocking anymore. They had ceased to observe common courtesies like leaving their shoes at the front door, and they no longer asked about wives or children, for their wives were all dead and their children all gone, the exception being the Calligrapher's son Dien, who was locked inside the kitchen every week during their gatherings because he was, as the Calligrapher put it, "shy," though the Poet and Guitarist and most of the Calligrapher's neighbors knew the real reasons.

Not once in two decades had the couch cushions been aired. The family altar stood neglected in the corner, bearing dusty photographs of the Calligrapher's late wife and an assortment of other ancestors. The only objects in the room that received regular cleaning were the framed paintings on the wall. There were about fifteen in total, ranging from envelope-sized to nearly five feet in diameter, each covered in abstract-looking black smears and accompanied by explanatory plaques with descriptions like "Pine Grove at Dawn," or "Woman in the Mist," or "Buffalo at the Foot of the Mountain." Supposedly the titles were also written in hidden Chinese characters within the paintings. All of them were signed at the bottom left corner, not with a name, but with a fingerprint.

The responsible finger was currently pointed in an accusatory manner in the Guitarist's direction.

"You! You lost the beat again!" The Calligrapher crumpled the page in front of him with his non-inky fist and threw it to the corner of the room with the other wadded-up paintings that he had rejected earlier in the evening. "How am I supposed to paint when you keep rhythm like a . . . like a . . . like . . ." He turned and looked expectantly at the Poet.

The Poet lifted his head from its resting place atop his multiple chins and thought for a moment. Taking advantage of the pause, the Guitarist removed the glove from his right hand and put it on his very cold left one.

"Like the way Old Nhan dances?" the Poet eventually supplied. Old Nhan was the Calligrapher's one-legged neighbor. Land mine, 1972. The accident was only ever spoken of indirectly.

"Exactly!" snorted the Calligrapher. "Now, have we finished with our mistakes?"

The Guitarist bobbed his head, but the Poet adopted a melancholy countenance and sighed. "Is one ever finished with one's mistakes?" he asked. Then, pleased with the line, he pulled a pencil and small, leather-bound notebook from his tweed jacket and wrote it down. Meanwhile, the Calligrapher had uncapped the vodka on the table and poured out four shots in swift succession. The first he drank. The second he gave to the Guitarist. The Poet took the third. And the final glass of vodka was emptied straight into the pot of ink. The Calligrapher gave it several good stirs with his pinky, then tapped the droplets off on the rim of the pot and licked the residue from his finger. The Guitarist switched glove hands again and readied his instrument. The Poet tucked his notebook back into his tweed jacket and sat up straighter. Painstakingly, the Calligrapher selected a piece of paper from the stack in front of him. First he inspected both sides, flipping it, examining the way the light hit its surface, bringing the sheet to his nose and sniffing it several times. Finally satisfied, he dipped his finger into the inkpot—the index finger this time—and drew it out slowly. There was a collective inhalation.

Now, up until this point all of the usual elements were aligned; the scene that followed should have been the one that played out every week. What came before—the banter, the crumpled paintings, the berating of the Guitarist—was all part of the routine. Once the vodka was half gone they did not make errors. The Calligrapher and the Guitarist should have moved their fingers simultaneously, the Calligrapher making sooty dabs on the paper while the Guitarist began to pluck his strings. Gradually, through a symbiosis that none of them had ever understood, a melody would emerge as the streaks of ink began to take form, the song and the painting inspiring each other. And then the Poet, listening and watching, would be moved to verse. They believed that it was this union of the three—the music, the painting, the words—that, like the blending of the finest strains of tea, could produce art in its most perfect form. Though, truthfully, the three men were barely artists. The Guitarist was the Electrician all the other days of the week, and the Poet had only ever published some of his racier poems and short stories in the lower-class magazines in Hanoi. The Calligrapher had never sold any of his paintings, but he had never tried to sell them, either. The three of them cared only about the process that took place when they gathered in the Calligrapher's living room, this collective act of organic creation. It had been this way since the late seventies, when they had begun their meetings because they were unable to give up the bond they had shared as soldiers. Art had replaced war as their act of communion.

But tonight, what should have happened did not. Tonight, just as the Calligrapher went to press his finger to the paper, he glanced up at the window behind the couch where the Poet was seated. At once his face went pale and he flinched violently, slashing the ink across the page and setting off a chain of physical reactions in the other two: Startled by the Calligrapher's aberrant movement, the Guitarist snapped a string loudly. At the twang, the Poet flinched and kicked out a plump leg, knocking the vodka bottle off the table, at which point it smashed on the tile floor. The sound of the shattering reached Dien in the kitchen, where he had been in his usual position— crouched beneath the sink and rocking back and forth. The noises aroused his curiosity and he crept over to the door to peer out through the keyhole, even though his eyesight wasn't very good. Dien had learned how to pick the lock years ago, but with only one good hand it was a laborious process. His left arm was about six inches longer than his right, the joints misaligned and the entire limb floppy in an unsettling way, but the fingers were rigid, underdeveloped stubs, fused together at their base. "Eel-arm," the Poet referred to it in private. Still, Dien had fared better than his two older brothers: Both were born dead, one with a small pair of extra arms on his chest that resembled the wings of a plucked chicken, and the other without eyes or nostrils.

In the living room, the Guitarist was preoccupied with his broken string and the Poet was staring at the paper on the table, troubled by the Calligrapher's uncharacteristic mistake but also thinking that there was not much difference between the ruined painting, the ones crumpled in the corner, and the ones that hung on the wall. The disruption of their routine had made the two of them uneasy. But the Calligrapher had now recovered his composure. He rose to his feet, his face calm, showing no sign either of the alarm that had possessed him a moment ago or embarrassment because of it. His fingers drummed against his thigh as he walked down the hallway to the kitchen.

Through the keyhole, Dien saw him coming and began rocking on his heels again. He bit his tongue. The Calligrapher paused before the door and said, keeping his voice even, "*Con*, your father is coming in to get the broom now." After waiting a few moments more, he selected one of the keys on the chain around his neck. But the instant the Calligrapher touched the doorknob, Dien released a long, hoarse scream and the Calligrapher jerked his hand back.

The Poet and the Guitarist tried not to look toward the kitchen, but the Guitarist turned his head when, a few seconds after the initial scream, they heard low groans and a thumping sound, which he guessed was the sound of Dien beating his head against a cupboard. The two men did not look at the Calligrapher when he came back into the living room without the broom. He did not resume his seat on the floor, and instead paced back and forth in front of the table, toying with a shard of broken bottle that he had picked up. Over and over and over he turned it in his inky fingers.

"Look outside and tell me what you see," he said to the Poet without looking up from the piece of glass. Struggling to accommodate the folds of his stomach, the Poet twisted to comply. The window faced east, away from the town.

"Hills. And darkness," said the Poet.

"Hills and darkness," murmured the Calligrapher. And stretching beyond them was more of the same. He knew those hills, that darkness, well. They all did. They knew the jungle that lay in that darkness, knew the spiders that were the size of ripe bananas and the rain that fell in torrents heavy enough to stun men too slow to find shelter. They knew the mist that came afterward. In those wild places time worked strangely, taking the shape of tree roots, warping and splitting and doubling back on itself until it was impossible to see where it really began. Forty years ago the three were young men running through those trees. Skinny things, hip bones jutting through green uniforms, they chased an enemy they could not see, and who could not see them. Most of their time was spare, and they spent it imagining the girls they knew from their old villages naked. At night the Guitarist would bring out the instrument he'd found in an abandoned American camp—it really couldn't be called a guitar anymore; the soundboard was cracked, the neck wobbled, and its four remaining strings were held in place by toothpicks—and the entire troop would listen while he played and the Poet chanted along. They did not worry about the invisible enemy hearing them. The Calligrapher was regularly hired by the other soldiers for tattoos, which he applied in bluish-green pigment using fishhooks and a small hammer. He inked their skin with zodiac symbols, with names of sweethearts, with tough-sounding phrases that the Poet would make up, and sometimes with monstrous creatures from his own imagination.

"It's for protection," he reasoned to a sergeant who had seemed distraught upon finding a five-headed bat on his back instead of the Buddha he had commissioned.

"It will make you a fierce warrior," he said of an inking on a biceps that appeared to be half stork, half tortoise.

The effectiveness of that particular tattoo was to remain untested, for the troop never actually took part in combat. They tramped through the hills for almost three years, keeping their weapons loaded and their packs as dry as possible, ready to sacrifice themselves when the time came, but they somehow managed to miss every battle. They would follow orders to move camp only to hear on the radio a week later that an unplanned skirmish had taken place shortly after they'd left, or else they would arrive too late and resign themselves to picking through what remained. When the war ended and they emerged unscathed from the jungle, they were told that they were fortunate.

And here they were, the lucky ones, sitting in the Calligrapher's living room forty years later, in various stages of physical decay. They were not heroes then. They were nothing now. The Calligrapher stopped playing with the piece of glass and placed it on the table. With his mouth set in a grim line that twitched at its edges, he stepped carefully around the pool of spilled vodka and walked to the couch—the Poet, alarmed, shrank away from his friend as best as his waistless figure could manage—reached around behind it, and then threw the window wide open. The Poet and the Guitarist gasped in unison. And then they shivered as the cold found them.

"Hills and darkness," the Calligrapher repeated again, as he surveyed the landscape before him. Silence fell, and they all realized that Dien had stopped having his fit in the kitchen. The Poet also noticed, dismayed, that his breath was now visible, and the Guitarist switched glove hands again. The Calligrapher stood before the window for a long, quiet minute before returning to his old spot on the floor. The others watched him with trepidation, their teeth chattering, and wondered why his weren't.

"We are very old friends, aren't we?" the Calligrapher said, eyeing the two of them with something that wasn't reassuring enough to be termed a smile. "Very old, very good friends?"

The Guitarist gave what could have been either a shiver or

a nod, but it must have been good enough for the Calligrapher, for he continued: "We are linked to one another by our memories, by our craft, by our secrets . . . I would do anything for either of you, anything that you asked. And I would do it no matter the sacrifice required. For you are my only family." He was back to knee-jiggling with a vengeance.

The Guitarist huddled on his wooden stool in mute bewilderment, but the Poet, who was better at dealing with words, spoke up: "Enough. We don't understand what it is you're on about. Are you satisfied?"

"I don't need you to understand, just to listen," said the Calligrapher. He placed the lid firmly on his pot of ink. "Though we have done nothing especially strange this evening, it appears that the strangeness has finally discovered us. Tonight I must tell you a story. A short story, but one that I have tried to keep a secret for a long time. If in the past I accidentally revealed pieces of it, it was done with these," he said, holding up his left hand and letting the splotchy fingers wave like the tendrils of a tide-pool–dwelling creature. "But I will not be using them to speak anymore." Still keeping the hand aloft, the Calligrapher turned to the Guitarist. "Begin with E minor. You won't need your broken B string. In fact, it will probably sound better without it." A long pause. And then, impatiently: "What are you waiting for?" The very confused Guitarist adjusted the instrument on his knee. "The story takes place in E minor, G, and F," the Calligrapher continued. "But I can't tell you the tune. Change chords when it feels right. There might be an A minor as well, if the story ends the way I hope it will. I can't know for certain, because you control a third of the telling. We are all following each other."

Next, he looked over at the Poet and grinned wickedly. "But for the moment all *you* are going to do is sit on your hands." The Calligrapher shushed him when he tried to protest. "If not, you'll try to close the window!" he reasoned.

"But the window *should* be closed! Something might come in!"

"That's exactly what I'm trying to avoid by leaving it open. Now do as I say before I come over there and force your hands under your great fat bottom myself." The Poet looked offended but obeyed, wiggling until his hands were underneath his thighs. Satisfied, the Calligrapher finally dropped his own stained left hand, and the Guitarist, though he was unaware that it was a cue, played an E minor chord as it fell. Behind the kitchen door, Dien's fingers shook as he inserted a skinny piece of wire into the lock and began coaxing it open.

"Bear in mind that I am working in an unfamiliar medium," began the Calligrapher. "My stories are painted, not spoken, and usually only spirits can loosen my tongue. But"—he gestured to the broken bottle on the floor—"tonight our other, very old, very good friend has fallen, so we must carry on without him as best we can." On his stool in the corner, the Guitarist changed from E minor to F and strummed slowly.

"We are all of us old and soft and mostly useless now, but I want you to try and picture the place about ninety-five miles north of here that they now call Empty Mountain. It was foggy and green and indistinguishable from the other mountains that surrounded it until the Americans sprayed it with their chemicals and the forest went dead. Think. Think! Yes, you see it clearly, even though four decades have passed since the three of us were stationed on its southeastern slope. We would have barely known each other, having just come out of the training camp. We were eager, but mostly we were young. Young and terrified. That is the part you may have forgotten. Remember it now.

"The night our story takes place was, like tonight, inauspiciously cold. Any of us could have been assigned to lookout, but that particular evening the watch fell to me. Though I was no more than ten or fifteen yards away from the camp where you and the others slept, the tents were only just visible in the insufficient moonlight. I stood alone at the point where jungle became deep jungle, my gun pointing at the shadows and shaking in my hands."

At this point the wind outside began blowing ever so slightly harder. The short bristly hairs on the back of the Poet's neck prickled. The Guitarist shuddered and began to alternate chords, picking four beats in G, four beats in E minor, then back again.

"I stared into that darkness and waited for something to emerge from it. I must have looked at it too long, too intently, too expectantly. What came out was something that I summoned myself. In the early hours of the morning, when my fear had still not abated but my eyes were beginning to droop, something in the jungle made a noise. A clicking. Soft, but distinctly non-animal in origin. *A monkey,* I told myself anyway. *It must be a monkey.* It grew louder, and it was coming from somewhere to my left. *A cricket then; a very large cricket,* I thought, but my trigger finger was twitching despite myself. Then the sound was coming from directly in front of me, and I saw a glimpse of something white and shapeless, flashing for a single instant out in the trees . . ."

The Calligrapher's voice trailed off, and for the first time in what felt like years he went completely still. His mouth when he spoke again barely seemed to move. "I fired."

At that very instant there was a single, sharp rap at the front door. The Guitarist came down hard on his E string, but it didn't break. For perhaps the third or fourth time this evening the Poet felt a pang of worry in his gut, for he knew that the Calligrapher never had guests apart from himself and the Guitarist.

But the Calligrapher just went on. "It was a single shot. I fired it without thinking. My eyes may even have been closed, for there was really no difference between the darkness of the jungle and the inside of my eyelids. I could hear perfectly, though. And after the crack of my gun, the fearful clicking stopped, and from the jungle I heard the sound of someone sighing."

There was another knock at the door.

"Aren't you going to see who it is?" asked the Poet.

"Ignore it," said the Calligrapher. "We must finish the story."

"Damn the story and answer your door!" the Poet blustered, but he remained sitting on his hands on the couch.

The Calligrapher's face was serene. "It is not necessary. I am perfectly aware of who is knocking, and you will be, too, if you stop interrupting me. Pay no attention to the door. There is no door. We are in the jungle and we are twenty-three years old and it is colder than we could have ever imagined. Out of fear I shot a bullet into the shadows and out of stupidity I decided to follow it. The sigh was a human one, I was certain, and every bit of me trembled as I felt my way through the dark to where I thought the sound had come from. E minor and F now . . . Good.

"I didn't notice the dying girl until she was practically underneath my feet, though at that point I wasn't yet aware that she was a girl—there was only enough moonlight to tell that what I had been about to stumble over was a pair of pale legs, not to whom they belonged. It sighed once more. I counted to one hundred and then, having convinced myself that I was being brave, put my gun away and grabbed hold of the ankles. They were cold and without pulse and, I assumed, attached to a body that was thoroughly dead. With heavy steps I began making my way out of the forest, dragging my find behind me. I didn't look back at it once; I kept my head up and my eyes fixed on the distant point where I knew camp was.

"But when the trees started thinning and letting the moonlight in, I realized that I was mistaken. The darkness had deceived me; I had gone trudging off in the wrong direction and emerged in an unfamiliar clearing. More frustrated than afraid now, I threw the legs down on the ground. It was then that the body sighed once again."

Here the knocking returned, and this time it escalated into a heavy pounding. The Poet suddenly leapt up. "It's Dien!" he cried. "He must have gotten out and needs to be let in again!"

The Calligrapher's nostrils twitched. He needed to shout to be heard over the banging at the door. "Sit back down! Dien is in the kitchen! You know perfectly well that he can't get out! Sit down! Down!" The knocking ended abruptly just as he said his final "down," and the word echoed around the room. The Poet dropped back onto the couch once more. "And your hands?"

The Poet muttered under his breath and settled back into position.

The Calligrapher was growing impatient. When he thought the Poet and the Guitarist wouldn't notice, his eyes darted up to the open window. "Please try and concentrate, for we are running out of time. Imagine, if you will, the chill of fear that ran through me as, at last, I turned to look at who I had shot.

"Her eyes were open, and the wound below her right breast wasn't bleeding as much as I expected. Now, you won't like what I'm going to say next. A young woman meeting her untimely end in the primeval forest, the young soldier responsible for her death dropping to his knees in anguish beside her—it is terrible, yes, but is it not darkly beautiful as well? And wouldn't you expect the star of this tragedy, the girl taking her final breaths in the moonlight, to be just as beautiful? As delicate as the dying sighs from her lips—which themselves ought to have been soft and fresh, full yet innocent—her slender limbs arranged in the tall grass as gracefully as those of a dancing Apsara. That was how she should have been.

"So you must not fault me for my reaction upon seeing her. Following my feelings of guilt and horror, of course, was disappointment. First, the girl was dressed in a bizarre harlequin ensemble of a tunic and short baggy trousers stitched together from orange scraps of what I recognized as parachute cloth. It was an outfit altogether ill-befitting a beautiful corpse. Even worse, her bare feet were so caked with mud that they had taken on the appearance of hooves, and her hands were almost as dirty and rather spade-shaped. The romanticism could have been saved had she possessed a lovely face, but in that category, too, she fell short. There was nothing fragile or pretty about her features; the girl's face was broad and squashy—almost like a pancake, with little slits for eyes and nostrils, and a pair of thick, unrefined lips toward the bottom. I couldn't help but feel as if I had been cheated somehow. The two of you think me beastly no doubt for saying this, but had it been you, you would have felt the same.

"My homely corpse blinked her small eyes at me. Her fleshy lips parted and she said, in a voice as flat as her face, 'So, you have killed me.' She sighed again and looked up at me with an expression of disappointment so powerful it rivaled what I was feeling inside—an expression that seemed to say, *I don't mind being shot, but why did you have to be the one to do it?*

"Naturally I was offended, but did I let it show? Of course

not. I said, with the perfect amount of tremor, 'It was an accident! An unforgivable accident that will haunt me for the
rest of my days and—'

"She cut me off abruptly. 'You can count on that,' she said
with something disarmingly like humor.

"I had been prepared to launch into my act of contrition. I
was going to weep and beat my fists against the ground and
then end by vowing to bring her body to her family and will-
ingly accept whatever punishment they chose to mete out.
However, at this interruption I began to lose my zeal. She
really wasn't cooperating at all. But I could have returned to
my heartbreaking plea for forgiveness had the dying girl not
done what she did next: She looked at me with disdain, pure
and unmistakable, and then she laughed. She laughed! Deri-
sive laughter that wouldn't stop even as it sent more blood
seeping out of her bullet wound. It was completely inappropri-
ate for a situation like this. Perverse, even.

" 'Look here,' I said, unable to keep the sulk out of my
voice, 'I'm rending my heart, trying to get an apology out before you exsanguinate, and you're not even listening!'

"She stopped laughing. It was clear that she hadn't liked
my tone. 'No, *you* look here, soldier,' she said. She was as rude
as she was ugly. 'Can I even call you "soldier"? You're an in-
sect that they plucked from a rice paddy and then handed a
gun. A mosquito larva, perhaps. Soldiers. You're useless, all of
you. I've been living right here, under your noses, unnoticed
for weeks now. I've had a front-row seat from which to observe your ineptness. I can only assume that you were able to

shoot me because you were aiming for something ten yards to my left.' Now that she was insulting me she seemed to be enjoying herself, but I couldn't help but notice happily that her breaths were growing shallower by the second.

" 'Hurry up and die, won't you?' I grumbled.

"The girl suddenly reached out, grabbed on to my ankle, and began tugging at it. 'I'm on my way,' she said, 'Come closer. Come down here with me.' I crouched next to her, wrinkling my nose at her particular musk. She looked up at me, and in each eye there was a little pinprick of moonlight. 'Soldier,' she said, 'someday you will regret what transpired here tonight. Because I am going to return and make sure of it. Oh, don't look like that! You deserve it, wouldn't you agree? You shot me and then you strayed where you should not. If you enter the woods, you shouldn't be surprised when something follows you out, that is, if you make it out at all.' A sharp, final sigh. 'I'm almost gone now. Quickly, give me your hand.'

"I remember thinking: *At last! She is frightened to move from this world to the next and needs me to comfort her in these last moments.* I went to take her hand, but to my surprise she reached out and grabbed mine first. Though she was weakened, her grip was formidable. She held my hand up in front of her eyes, as if inspecting it. Then she pushed all the digits down into a fist except for the index, which she left out pointing right at her own face.

" 'Here is the finger that did it,' she whispered. 'Here is the one that pulled the trigger.' And then, in what was to be her last act on earth, she bit down on it as hard as she could.

"She had the jaws of a tiger. I shrieked and slapped her repeatedly with my free right hand, but I was entirely ineffective; she only unclamped her teeth when she was finally dead, fifteen very long, very painful seconds later. I cradled my poor finger in the fabric of my shirt and tried to stanch the bleeding; the flesh was shredded, and I didn't appear to have knuckle skin anymore, but luckily she hadn't bitten hard enough to sever the member.

"I kicked the body of the no-longer-dying girl twice before leaving her there. You don't need to make that face; I know it wasn't very civil. But that wasn't the worst thing I did. When I saw how her face was now covered in the blood from my mangled finger, I thought to myself that it was a vast improvement. Yes, yes, you may look horrified."

The Calligrapher paused and bestowed a meaningful glance upon each of his friends. "Now here is the part where the story becomes a bit implausible," he said.

This time it was the Guitarist's turn for an outburst. "You mean that everything else *was* believable?" he cried. For emphasis, he viciously strummed an E minor seventh.

The Calligrapher looked up over the Guitarist's shoulder at one of his prized pieces hanging on the wall. The title on the frame identified it as *The Path Out of the Forest,* but to the untrained eye it would appear to be no more than a collection of vertical smudges. While the Calligrapher's attention was diverted, the Poet shifted his weight to free one of his hands. He surreptitiously pulled out his notebook and pencil again, and on a fresh page wrote: "One-Finger" in neat cursive. The Calligrapher, who did not take his eyes off his painting once, surely couldn't have noticed the Poet's furtive movements, but a curious smile crossed his face when the Poet quietly slipped his notebook back into his pocket. Still staring at *The Path Out of the Forest*—though it seemed more as if he were staring through it—the Calligrapher brought his part of the story to an end.

"I began walking through the trees, confident that I would soon emerge at the forest's edge. Every few steps I stopped to tear the leaves off the ferns growing in the underbrush and bandage myself with them. Eventually the task absorbed me, and my attention wandered away from the more pressing matter of getting back to camp. It was only when I had forgotten about finding my way out that I was able to do so. I looked up from wrapping another leaf around my finger to discover that I was somehow back at my original lookout post. There was camp, fifteen yards away from me once more—a cluster of geometric shadows beneath the moon, which was now starting to set. Though I wanted nothing more than to drag myself back to my tent and lose myself in sleep, the night was not yet over, and I knew what was expected of me: I resumed my position and stood staring into the darkness for the hours of it that remained.

"When dawn broke I was relieved from the watch by Pimple-Face Quan. You both remember him—he was the one who killed a monkey with his bare hands on a dare from Crooked-Nose Thanh. When Pimple-Face Quan saw the blood on my clothes he looked concerned, but I didn't provide an explanation and he didn't press for one. I ran off to wash before you and all the others rose, and to think up a decent lie to account for my injury. As I approached the stream by camp I remember thinking that either my makeshift plant-cast had been effective or the cold night had numbed the pain, because my finger was barely throbbing anymore.

"When I was certain that I was not being observed, I slowly unwrapped the bandage to see what damage the dead girl's teeth had done. In the light of day there could be no mistake: There was still plenty of blood on the digit, dried and dark, but the skin underneath it was now unbroken. I washed away the carnage and examined it again—there were no marks, no marks at all. As I gaped at my own finger incredulously, the last of the pain left my body. It still didn't feel *right,* and it never really would again. But after a time I resigned myself to the belief that what had transpired during the night had all been in my head. Why have you stopped playing?"

The Guitarist had not moved his hands for a long time. The Poet's were now folded in his lap instead of beneath him. He looked at the Calligrapher and asked, in the voice that he used with child beggars, gentle but measured, "Why are you telling us this?"

Only now did the Calligrapher look away from his painting. "Because, dear friends, earlier this evening I was startled to see a familiar, unattractively flat, blood-covered face looking in at us from that very window. It is my guess that after all these years, she has returned to carry out the promise she made to me in the forest." Both the Poet and the Guitarist did not let themselves turn to look outside. The Calligrapher's voice dropped to a low snarl. "However, I don't intend to let her."

"And what, precisely, are you planning to do?" asked the Poet wearily.

"Well," said the Calligrapher, "this is the part where your cooperation is necessary." Still seated, he reached around and from somewhere behind his back drew out a large kitchen knife.

"Good God!" the Guitarist yelped, and rocked backward on his stool.

The Poet did not want to dwell on the reasons why his friend had been hiding a knife this entire time. "Why don't I take that from you?" he said softly. "Why don't you hand it to me, very carefully?"

The Calligrapher presented it to him politely, handle first, without complaint. "Excellent. Take it," he said. "For I need you to use it to cut off my finger."

"What?!"

"My left index. One of you must amputate it." When this was met with silence that was more exasperated than stunned, he calmly continued: "Don't you see? The trigger finger that she didn't manage to destroy in the forest—it must be sacrificed in order to atone for what I did. It is the only way to appease her. It's why she tracked me down. Listen . . ."

The knocking at the door was back again, soft but insistent. Almost like a gentle scratching now, which was somehow more frightening.

"I had hoped that our fallen comrade would be able to assist us in this task," said the Calligrapher, indicating the broken vodka bottle, "to make it easier. Because the truth is that I am a coward." He rose to his knees and placed his left hand atop the stack of paper on the table. "I cannot do it myself." He spread his fingers wide and lifted his chin. His fingers were steady. "Who is my true friend? Which of you will help me?"

The Poet raised the knife, reflecting a blurry, distorted living room in the blade. He placed it on the table next to the Calligrapher's hand and shook his head. The Calligrapher turned to look at the Guitarist, but the stool was now empty; the Guitarist was in the corner, putting his instrument back in its case.

The Poet lifted himself from the couch cushions. "Don't take this the wrong way, Cong," he said. "We're not calling you a liar, but Liem and I think that you might need, well, a *rest*. Didn't you say it yourself earlier, that we are all old and soft and useless?" He tugged the waistband of his trousers up. "I, too, can sometimes feel a little lost in my own mind. Perhaps it's all for the best that our drink took a tumble earlier. Just rest tonight, Cong, and we'll see you next week." He went to stand by the Guitarist.

"I understand," said the Calligrapher. "You are free to leave." He made a grand gesture toward the front door. "I believe that you both know the way out . . ."

The Poet and the Guitarist followed the sweep of his arm with their eyes, but neither of them moved; the soft knocking had not gone away. They looked at each other nervously.

The Calligrapher clapped with undisguised glee. "You

see!" he cried. "There is a part of you that believes me and you know it! If there wasn't, you would have been through that door already. But you can't help but wonder if she's waiting out there, can you? It frightens you, even if it's not you she wants. So will you march out that door and meet her, just to prove that you are not afraid? Or will you admit that you are and stay? She is patient—she has been waiting for me these forty years already. If you don't help me, dear friends, we may be killing time here for quite a while."

The Guitarist shuffled his feet. The Poet's eyes darted from the door to the Calligrapher, from the Calligrapher to the door. He had reached a decision. A look of defiance came over his face as he hoisted his trousers once more. "This means nothing!" he declared. And then he turned, stepped onto the couch (a motion that caused its middle to sag to the floor), and heaved himself up and out of the window. There was a small thud as he landed in the soft earth of the Calligrapher's garden five feet below.

The Guitarist shrugged and then mounted the couch, too. He handed the guitar case down to the Poet below, and then swung one leg over the windowsill.

Before he jumped he heard the voice of the Calligrapher. "Perhaps if you had played an A minor this could have ended differently," was what he said. And then the Guitarist was gone, too, old bones clicking as he hit the ground and started running down the back roads that led away from the house, the Poet huffing and puffing alongside him with the guitar clutched to his chest.

The Calligrapher placed his inky hand back on the table. He balled all of the fingers save for the index into a fist. He was ready now. "Come in," he said softly. With his right hand he picked up the knife and placed it on the floor. Then, with a little flick, he sent it sliding across the tile and toward the entrance to the kitchen. It spun to a stop mere feet from where Dien was pressed against the wall of the dark hallway, listening. "Come in," called the Calligrapher once more. As a cold mountain breeze crossed in through the window with a sigh, Dien detached himself from the shadows. With his good arm he reached for the knife on the ground, or perhaps he was reaching for the twisted version of the living room reflected in its blade. Whichever it was, when he held it in his hand, he knew what was expected of him.

DESCENDING DRAGON

——

Ms. Nguyen was having her daily phone conversation with her daughter Lam when she saw the first tank. It appeared abruptly in the middle of her bedroom, enormous and yellow-green, its treads caked with red Mekong mud and its long gun resting on the windowsill less than two feet away from her. For five long seconds the tank quietly occupied the space before her. It somehow put the other objects in the room slightly out of focus, making everything else seem unreal by comparison. She was less surprised by the appearance of the tank than by the fact that she did not fear it, as she would have forty years ago. It even smelled the same way she remembered—like dust and buffalo shit, with something tangy and metallic underneath—and even though Ms. Nguyen knew it was a hallucination, she had the urge to get up and touch it. She didn't, though, because Lam's voice suddenly trilled in the earpiece. Her daughter had always been a little too perceptive, too good at detecting the minute shifts in atmosphere that indicated when something was wrong. And Ms. Nguyen's silence now, at the appearance of the tank, though brief, had already triggered Lam's suspicions:

"*Mẹ? Mẹ?* Mom? Are you there?"

At the sound of Lam's voice, the tank disappeared. Not instantly, as it had appeared, but in pieces, like a puzzle disassembling: The muddy wheels vanished first, and then the hull, leaving the gun hanging in the air by itself. Then Ms. Nguyen blinked, and it too was gone. She tightened her hold on her telephone with one hand and gripped the edges of the stiff, upholstered armchair with the other, anchoring herself in the physical world. When she spoke her voice was steady: "Yes. I am sorry; I am losing my attention so easily these days."

Though Lam said nothing, her mother could hear her shifting uncomfortably in her chair on the other side of the line. Ms. Nguyen smiled and continued: "The shaking came back today, *con,* so the nurse had to dial your number for me. And I have new pains in my knees. I ate lunch with Mrs. Phillips and she thinks that my cough is becoming worse."

Lam exhaled and said, "*Mẹ,* I—"

Ms. Nguyen continued as if she could not hear her daughter: "But don't worry yourself about me; I am sure that a little rest will take care of everything. That's all I need. A little rest. I haven't been sleeping well, you know. Sometimes I lie awake all night."

"*Mom!*" Lam's voice was shrill and pleading. "There's something I need to tell you."

"I am always listening, *con*."

"I can't fly down for Lunar New Year like we planned."

Ms. Nguyen was silent. She could tell that her daughter was choosing her words very carefully.

"Plane tickets aren't cheap, Mom, and it's going to be a bad week at work. I really can't take off. I'm sorry, *Mẹ*."

Ms. Nguyen pressed her lips together tighter.

"Please, Mom, I just saw you over Christmas, and I'm flying down for Easter, so I'll see you soon. I just can't for *tết*."

"Oh, *con*," Ms. Nguyen said at last. "Did you know, my feet are always cold now?"

Lam sighed. "Then you should wear the wool socks that I sent you, *Mẹ*."

"They are very slippery, *con*."

After she hung up the phone, Ms. Nguyen stood and walked slowly and deliberately around the entire room before sitting down again. She realized that she was probably losing her mind, and felt a little shiver of delight.

UNLIKE THE OTHER WOMEN in the St. Ignatius Assisted Living Facility, Ms. Nguyen never mourned for her lost past. Her fellow residents still longed for the 1950s and '60s, when they were wasp-waisted Houston housewives. Those sun-drenched days: clean, ruddy-cheeked children climbing the live oak trees and pecan pies cooling on windowsills. The world was different now—these women had become little more than swollen-heeled bags of bones—but they still dyed their limp hair biweekly and daubed dark eye shadow onto wrinkled lids for dinner in the cafeteria or for bingo night. They kept their old dresses in their closets: slinky gowns cut in velvet and satin that smelled like cigarette smoke and old oil money. They turned their dressers into shrines, covering them with black-and-white photographs of their younger, smiling selves.

Unlike them, Ms. Nguyen did not court memory. She was relatively young for a resident but as wizened as the best of them, and wore her wrinkles, her liver spots, and the stoop in her back with something like grace. Looking at her it was impossible to envision the young girl that she must have once been. But Ms. Nguyen had her ghosts. She had tried to leave them on the other side of the Pacific, but they had followed her at a distance, never quite letting her out of their sight. And now that she lived at St. Ignatius, where she spent the long days in an easy chair, watching the hours limp slowly by, they were becoming harder to ignore. The mind drifted away too easily here; the walls were all bare and cream-colored, and in this blankness the memories crept in. They lapped at the edge of her consciousness like the Mekong, deep and patient and full of silt, and soaked into her dreams. There were good ghosts—the breeze that made the rice stalks dance, the snort of her father's water buffalo, the way the sunlight would make a halo on her mother's black hair—but there were many more bad ones: the shrieking sound of exploding shells in the night, the dried blood in the street gutters, the hissing sound of a soldier's fly unzipping, his shadow obscuring a figure curled on her side on the ground . . .

Ms. Nguyen had not feared the tank. But because it had found its way into this world, materializing in front of her in broad daylight, she feared that the other ghosts would soon follow.

She spent the time before dinner in a state of extreme alertness, wondering if she would see it again. While she waited, she examined in minute detail the state of her cracked, yellowed fingernails and the pattern of blue veins that rose in ridges on the backs of her hands. She imagined that she could feel things shifting and creaking underneath her skin. At five thirty she rose from her chair and left her room, noting with satisfaction the various clicks and groans her body made as it slowly settled into an upright position. She viewed each new pain, each new corporeal malfunction that indicated another teetering step down the path of senility, with a twisted joy. Her first hot flash had been more exciting to her than her first period, and she was anticipating the day when she would get a cane. In the mornings when she dressed herself she would sometimes catch a glimpse of her own hunched back in the mirror and smile. As she made her way toward the elevator, she calculated in her head the time difference between America and Vietnam. It was very early in the morning there. When she passed the front staircase on her way down the hallway, she let one hand rest briefly on the carved rail of the banister. To her, the stairs were more alive than anything else in this place.

St. Ignatius was a square, ugly concrete building, colored in chromes and dirty pinks and teals and linoleum marked gray from skidding wheelchairs, but the front staircase was its one feature of aesthetic note—it was a relic from some earlier, lovelier time, high and curving and made from a dark, lustrous sort of wood. It was mostly for show; nearly all of the residents relied solely on the elevator to move from floor to floor. Had the facility been larger, or wealthier, the staircase would have been declared a safety hazard and consequently remodeled and fitted with handrails, wheelchair lifts, and emergency buttons. But St. Ignatius—much like the residents it housed—was forgotten and falling apart, and no safety inspectors came, and the tall staircase, with its naked, uneven wood, remained.

For the residents who could still chew, dinner was corn bread, okra, a flabby turkey cutlet, and an unnaturally yellow slice of lemon meringue pie. Things were still, save for the chomping of fifty pairs of elderly teeth and the ceiling fan shuffling around the stale air. Alone at her table, Ms. Nguyen ate slowly. She still had all her teeth, but they would probably be gone in a couple of years, she reasoned.

Sometimes she liked to talk to herself while she ate. But unlike the residents who yelled obscenities at invisible beings, heard voices, and drooled uncontrollably, when Ms. Nguyen held her mad conversations with herself they were always calm, polite, and in Vietnamese, which seemed to disturb the nursing staff even more.

"I've heard about people going back, as tourists," she was saying that evening, holding her fork up to the light so that the tines reflected it. "To Vietnam, I mean. Back to the motherland. But how can they stand it now that everything is changed?" She paused, then nodded as if receiving a response. "I would only go back to see Ha Long Bay again. Ha Long has been the same for centuries; it will be the same for centuries to come. Have I ever told you the story of Ha Long?" She waited again. "No? I used to tell it to Lam, when she was a child. You see, long ago, a dragon fell from the sky. It broke the ground where it landed, broke it into a thousand islands. When it—"

She was interrupted by a commotion by the doors. Mrs. Gaston, a hefty woman of seventy-five, who, last week, had tripped over her own walker and fractured a metatarsal, was entering the cafeteria with her foot in a cast, pushed in a wheelchair by her son and followed by a parade of grandchildren. Ms. Nguyen's initial displeasure at the disruption suddenly disappeared—she had an idea. She did not say another word for the remainder of dinner, and all the nurses breathed a sigh of relief.

EARLY THE NEXT MORNING, as the sun rose, Ms. Nguyen stood at the top of the stairs wearing her pajamas and the pair of thick, gray woollen socks that had been a present from Lam. She wriggled her toes inside them; for the first time in a long while, her feet felt warm. Ms. Nguyen swayed a little, feeling the surface slide beneath her socks. It tickled slightly. She needed the correct kind of accident—the hip, ideally, or the ankle. A wrist might not be adequate. She swayed again, more intensely. Perhaps the staircase wasn't steep enough. But she knew she had to act soon—the cleaning ladies would be arriving within the hour. She was not afraid.

Ms. Nguyen bent her knees and felt short of breath. Sunlight was crawling through the windows, turning the world white again. She let go of the banister. The old ghosts were flooding in, and Ms. Nguyen realized as she leapt that she was falling into their waiting arms. In the space of time between her toes leaving the landing and her body crumpling as it hit the floor at the bottom, she looked through the front window and saw that the tank was back, planted triumphantly in the middle of the lawn, glowing reddish in the early morning sun. It did not belong here, but neither did she.

Ms. Nguyen lay sprawled on her left side, with her leg bent at a strange new angle beneath her. She decided that it might be a good idea to begin yelling but discovered that her mouth was already open; tears were on her face, and people were running toward her. She heard herself making loud, animal yelps, and the sound surprised her. But by the time the medic came, Ms. Nguyen had calmed herself down enough to inquire when her daughter would be arriving.

ACKNOWLEDGMENTS

———

FOR THEIR SUPPORT, patience, and guidance, my deepest gratitude goes to: Cindy Spiegel, Molly Friedrich, Lucy Carson, and Molly Schulman; Don Weber and the sage members of the Mount Holyoke College English Department; the Pham, the Block, and the Kupersmith clans; and the friends scattered from Yorkshire Road to South Hadley, from London to the Mekong Delta.

And to Valerie Martin, for everything.

PHOTO: © SARAH PENNIMAN

VIOLET KUPERSMITH was born in rural Penn-sylvania in 1989 and grew up outside of Philadelphia. Her father is American and her mother is a former boat refugee from Vietnam. After graduating from Mount Holyoke College, Kupersmith received a yearlong Ful-bright Fellowship to teach and research in the Mekong Delta. She is currently at work on her first novel.

www.VioletKupersmith.com